Books by Joy Reed

Seraphina Fox Mysteries

The Ghost in the Machine

Poison in Jest

All Hallows' Eve

Night Music

The Hanged Man

Ministry of Angels

Published by Unconsidered Trifle Publications

Historical Romances

An Inconvenient Engagement

Twelfth Night

The Seduction of Lady Carroll

Midsummer Moon

Lord Wyland Takes a Wife

The Duke and Miss Denny

A Home for the Holidays

Lord Caldwell and the Cat

Miss Chambers Takes Charge

The Baron and the Bluestocking

Lord Desmond's Destiny

Lord Yates and the Yankee

Mr. Jeffries and the Jilt

Catherine's Wish

Emily's Wish

Anne's Wish

Published by Zebra Books

NIGHT MUSIC

BEING THE FOURTH VOLUME OF THE

MEMOIRS

OF

MADAME SERAPHINA FOX,

SPIRITUALIST,

DESCRIBING HER WORLDLY AND OTHERWORLDLY

EXPERIENCES

EDITED BY JOY REED, M.A., B.Sci.

ISBN: 0692116184
ISBN13: 9780692116180
Unconsidered Trifle Publications, Maumelle, AR

Dedicated to Gayle
(again and with interest)

Chapter 1

"Is there a disembodied spirit in the room?"

The question went unanswered—or at least received no answer that the ears could detect. But a close observer might have noticed a stirring of the velvet curtains and a flickering of the candle in the lantern overhead.

"Is there a disembodied spirit in the room?"

Once again, the words received no audible response. But another breath of air swept through the room, carrying with it the scent of pine: fresh and sharp and alien in the closed chamber.

"Henry," said Mrs. Toth, with considerable satisfaction.

Her son and daughter exchanged glances. There was more resignation than satisfaction in their manner. Mrs. Toth did not notice, however, for her gaze was fixed on the box in front of us. It was a wooden box about two feet long and half as wide, its edges bound and studded in brass like a steamer trunk. On the top surface was a large dial with the alphabet inscribed around its circumference.

"Is there a disembodied spirit in the room?"

As I spoke the question for the third time, I let a note of drama creep into my voice. And my words were answered by the chiming of a bell somewhere within the box.

"Henry," said Mrs. Toth again, just as I myself spoke: "Is this the spirit of Henry David Thoreau?"

The answer to both these remarks was another chime.

"Dear Henry," said Mrs. Toth, and smiled.

Her children kept their eyes fixed resolutely on the box. I, however, studied Mrs. Toth beneath my lashes, even as I had done a hundred times before. She had claims to beauty still, Dear Reader, for all that she was old enough to be a grandmother. Yet there was something repellent about her, too. Perhaps it was her fleshlessness—the fact that she was so thin as to be practically skeletal. Her hands, ornamented with fine rings, were all bone and sinew, and her pale eyes—not blue or grey, but some indeterminate colour in between—were deep-set above cheekbones that protruded like a death's head's.

Her views were as eccentric as her appearance. The wealthy widow of a New England manufacturer, Mrs. Toth was not only an exponent of Spiritualism, but of Socialism, Temperance, Vegetarianism, and half a dozen other -isms as well.

Her son and daughter were the fitting offspring of such a parent. Absalom Toth and his sister Ernestine were weedy and stoop-shouldered, with their mother's pale eyes and hair so fair as to be nearly colourless. Looking at them, I was always reminded of potatoes sprouted in a dark cellar. The description is not original to me, Dear Reader. Mrs. Gaskell used it first, in reference to the Brontë children and their strange insular upbringing. But I thought it equally suited to the Toths.

Mind you, they themselves would have scorned the comparison. And this despite the fact that they were Vegetarians—but Vegetarians of a very rarefied sort. That is to say, they would only eat what Mrs. Toth called "aspiring vegetables": vegetables that grew above the ground rather than in it. Likewise, they abjured milk, and eggs, and cereal grains, and all manner of other seemingly inoffensive foodstuffs.

Now I have nothing against Vegetarianism *per se,* Dear Reader. One may doubtless live a perfectly healthy life without consuming animal flesh. But to reject root vegetables—perhaps the most nutritious and sustaining of viands, as generations of Irish might attest—seemed to me akin to madness. In my opinion, it went a long way toward explaining the younger Toths' distinctly unhealthy appearance. But Mrs. Toth would never have dreamed of asking my opinion on such a subject. She wanted one thing from me and one thing only: the exercise of my powers at the séance table.

Those powers are justly famous, Dear Reader. Perhaps you, too, have heard of me.

My name is Seraphina Fox.

Or to use the title I claim on my card, I am *Madame Seraphina Fox, Spiritualistic Medium, Clairvoyant, and Inventor of the Electrical Spiritograph.*

Now if you have read any of my previous memoirs,[1] Dear Reader, you will know that my name is not really Seraphina Fox. That is the name I took upon coming to London some twelve years ago, in an effort to make a clean break with a scandalous past. You will also be aware that I am not a true Spiritualistic Medium and Clairvoyant, though that should go without saying. I am assuming that you, like me, are intelligent enough to realize

[1]*Ghost in the Machine, Poison in Jest,* and *All Hallows' Eve*

that when people claiming such titles are not out-and-out charlatans (like me), they are generally self-deluded fools.

As for the Electrical Spiritograph, that is admittedly as bogus as my psychic powers. But it has an impressive appearance, besides being an original development in the field of Spirit Communication. As a long-time player in the Spiritualism game, I can assure you that that is far more important. I am old enough to have participated in most of Spiritualism's major trends, from the table-rapping first popularized by the Fox sisters (from whom I took my surname) to the full-figure manifestations in vogue these last couple of decades.

Looking around for a new angle on the business, I soon realized that Science is all the rage nowadays. Hardly a schoolboy or -girl but has a collection of rocks or butterflies or some such thing, while you may hear servants, cabmen, and shopkeepers arguing over the theories of Mr. Darwin, just as in the halls of academia. In the same way, inventions like the telegraph have revolutionized our lives, bringing regular news from far-flung shores that would have taken weeks or months to arrive not so many years ago. What more appropriate, then, as a telegraph to communicate with that yet farther shore—the World beyond this one, or what we Spiritualists call the Summerland or Other Side?

Such was the inspiration for my Electrical Spiritograph. It is not very like a telegraph in appearance or operation, as you may have gathered. I have striven rather for simplicity in my design, to make the messages it delivers understandable to anyone. There is a bell to answer straightforward yes-and-no queries, and an alphabet dial to spell out longer messages.

My clients, being true Spiritualistic Believers, are convinced these messages come directly from the Other Side via Spirit Energy. That is my own pet theory, based on the widely-accepted notion that electricity pervades all life. According to the theory of Spirit Energy, Death does not destroy this electricity but rather converts it into a spiritual form, invisible to the eye but universally pervasive, and accessible to those who possess the means—which is to say, Mediumistic ability and an Electrical Spiritograph.[2]

But if you have read any of my previous memoirs, Dear Reader, you will know better than to believe this. If not, I will simply state here that my device is battery-powered rather than Spirit-powered. To make the bell ring or the wheel turn, I operate one of a pair of simple switches. As a precaution, there are two sets of these switches, one which I can operate with my feet, and another, less convenient set that I can operate with my thumbs in situations of extremity.[3] And there is also a master switch to cut power to the device altogether, should a major malfunction occur, such as is described in my first memoir.[4]

By this, you will see that I mean to deal truthfully with you, Dear Reader. No matter how I may deceive others, I will never try

---

[2] In positing that energy is not destroyed but only transmuted to another form after death, Madame Fox ingeniously draws upon the conclusions of her scientific contemporaries regarding the Law of Conservation of Energy and the First Law of Thermodynamics.—*Ed.*

[3] The Spiritograph is bolted to the table on which it sets. This table has four apparently solid legs and a central pedestal base, studded at intervals with brass studs. Madame Fox wears Turkish slippers with a surface of pure silver metal inset beneath their upturned toes. By pressing the toe of a slipper against a particular pair of the metal studs on the pedestal base, the circuit is completed. Metal rods running up through the table legs take the power to the box—and the end result is that the bell rings (in the case of the left slipper) or the wheel turns (in the case of the right). –*Ed.*

[4] *Ghost in the Machine*

to deceive you. And since you will, of necessity, encounter a great deal of deception in this, the affair of my fourth memoir, it should be a comfort to know that between you and me there will exist only the most perfect frankness—excepting only a slight, ladylike reticence in regard to strictly personal matters.

Returning, then, to the Toths: I must confess that, despite my much-vaunted psychic abilities, I had no inkling that evening that anything was about to change in our relationship. Mrs. Toth had been a client for several years now, to her own satisfaction and my own considerable profit. She was, as mentioned before, quite wealthy enough to indulge her eccentricities, of which she had any number. Only one need concern us here, however, and that is her passion for the late Henry David Thoreau, Naturalist, Transcendentalist, and (according to her) the long-lost lover of her youth.

It is quite possible that you have never heard of Henry David Thoreau, Dear Reader. Among the Transcendentalist philosophers, he never achieved the same fame as Ralph Waldo Emerson, his more celebrated countryman and sometime friend. For my part, I have come to believe Thoreau was the greater man of the two, possessing a fresh, original style that endears itself upon closer acquaintance. But even in his lifetime, his work was little noticed. Now that he has been dead for some decades, it is a struggle to find his works in his own country, let alone this one. I was obliged to employ American agents, and to represent myself as a potential English publisher, to obtain copies of his published books and essays along with transcripts of his unpublished journals.

Still, it was worth my while to do so. Mrs. Toth was willing to pay, and pay well, to converse with her Spiritual Spouse. That is how she referred to him, Dear Reader: her Spiritual Spouse. This was to distinguish him from her Earthly Spouse, the late Hiram Toth. Although the latter gentleman had given her his name, a lifetime's devotion, and—subsequently—all his worldly wealth, Mrs. Toth was accustomed to speak of him slightingly as a mere Materialist.

"If only I had been in a position to marry my dear Henry," she would often say, with a wistful look on her death's head countenance. "How different my life would have been! We were desperately in love, you know—quite desperately. But my parents forced me to accept Hiram's suit simply because he was so very rich. I was but seventeen at the time and quite unable to withstand the pressure that was put upon me. It has been a source of regret to me all my life. And of course it almost killed poor Henry. He became more and more of a recluse and ended by withdrawing from society altogether. It was so very sad—both our lives ruined by my parents' worldly ambitions."

Between you and me, Dear Reader, I regarded this story with extreme skepticism. There is evidence that Mr. Thoreau did tender his heart and hand unsuccessfully to one or two women during his lifetime, but I had never been able to discover that Irene Toth, neé Pinkley, was among them. If she was, I consider he had a narrow escape. You had only to look at her to know she was the kind of woman who would never be satisfied, no matter what her circumstances. If she had married the Transcendentalist rather than the Materialist, I was willing to bet she would have complained bitterly about his lack of worldly ambition and bewailed the more lucrative match she might have made with Mr. Toth.

I thought, too, that it was hard on her children to hear her continually regretting her marriage to their father. This was the more so because Mr. Toth had left all his money to her, making them dependent upon her for every penny.

Of course dependency is a relative thing, Dear Reader. Ernestine and Absalom Toth were fully grown adults now, being both in their mid-thirties. I, for one, could see no reason why they might not have supported themselves, especially since they were American and thus presumably free of the English prejudice against wage-earning. Indeed, I gathered that at some point Mr. Toth had actually pursued medical training with the idea of setting up as an Eclectic Physician. But that scheme had apparently come to nothing, and his sister's attempt to equip herself for life had consisted of a single, abortive semester at Oberlin College. They seemed content now to sit passively by, as their mother gave rein to her own frustrated ambitions.

That evening was quite typical of our sessions at the Spiritograph. "Henry," said Mrs. Toth, gazing tenderly down at the machine as if she beheld therein the countenance of her lover, "O Henry, do you remember that afternoon we spent on Walden Pond?"

Repressing a yawn, I spelled out "A C-O-N-J-U-N-C-T-I-O-N O-F S-O-U-L-S." Mrs. Toth often spoke of that afternoon on Walden Pond, Dear Reader—too often for my taste. According to her, Henry had taken her out in his boat and serenaded her with his flute as they had floated along, and they had been transcendently happy. She was circumstantial enough in the details to make me think there really had been some such episode, though I doubted whether it had held the significance she gave it. I felt I knew Mr. Thoreau pretty well by now, after studying his books and journals and letters, and I didn't believe he would have found anything to attract him in Mrs. Toth, even in her youthful prime.

But it is my job to please my clients, Dear Reader, which often means taking liberties with the feelings and opinions of their Dear Departed Ones. So when Mrs. Toth, with a sentimental sigh, said, "O Henry, I fear you would not recognize the girl you knew that day," I immediately responded, "T-H-E Y-E-A-R-S P-E-R-F-E-C-T A-N-D R-I-P-E-N H-E-R," apologizing mentally to Mr. Thoreau as I did so.

Mrs. Toth smiled with pleasure at these words. Once again her son and daughter glanced at her, then at each other. I thought they must be as weary of the whole business as I was, to judge by their expressions. Mrs. Toth must have noticed something amiss in their expressions, too, for she addressed her daughter sharply: "Is something wrong, Ernestine?"

"Nothing, Mother," said Miss Toth in a breathless little voice.

"And you, Absalom?" said Mrs. Toth, addressing her son in his turn. "Is something wrong?"

He hesitated, then spoke with an apologetic air. "You know I had accepted Charlie Welch's invitation to visit his club this evening, Mother. I did not realize then that we were planning to come here. If we are to be much longer . . .."

His voice trailed off as his mother, colour mounting to her hollow cheeks, responded more sharply still: "You can perfectly well wait until our sitting is finished, Absalom. I should hope you would not begrudge me a little happiness. When I consider all I have done for you and your sister, and the way you have repaid me—"

"Yes, of course, Mother," he said quickly, evidently hoping to stem the flood.

She, however, snapped, "Don't interrupt me! I *detest* being interrupted."

"Yes, Mother," he said, ducking his head like a chastened child. "I do apologize."

She regarded him for a moment, then turned away with a shrug. "I should hope so," she said. Glancing down at the Spiritograph, she added pettishly, "Indeed, you have spoiled the whole sitting. I daresay Henry will refuse to communicate any more tonight, after such an interruption."

And in fact he did, Dear Reader. Much as I hated to do it, I felt I had to take my cue from her. She was obviously expecting the Spiritograph to fall in with her mood, and—as stated before—it is my job to meet my clients' expectations, however uncongenial I might find them. In any case, the little exchange between her and her son had put a damper on things, from which I judged I did not have enough battery power left to recover. Of course it was hard lines on Mr. Toth, who had to bear the blame for bringing the sitting to a premature close. I smiled sympathetically at him by way of apology, as we all got up from the table and filed out of the Spirit Parlour.

In the corridor outside, Susan was waiting. Susan is my second-in-command and my chief partner in the Spiritualism business. She is a middle-aged woman with an appearance of quiet efficiency (which is real) and of staid respectability (which is not). She has been with me ever since I founded the Temple of Spiritualism and has, indeed, been a major factor in its success. Intelligent and capable, Susan can turn her hand to anything, be it impersonating a Spirit with a length of phosphorescent gauze or detecting a half-penny overcharge in a tradesman's account. By way of illustration, I will give you a resumé of her activities that evening:

When the Toths had first arrived, she had taken their coats and cloaks and Mr. Toth's hat, ushered them into the Sitting Room, and brought in a tray containing tea-cups and a pot of green tea. Normally we drink sherry in the interval that precedes the sitting, but the Toths, being Teetotalers, forced us to substitute this milder beverage.

While I was drinking tea with my clients, Susan had gone through their outer garments, checking the pockets for letters, receipts, or any other information that might be useful to us. And thanks to a timely note given me by Susan just before the séance began, Henry David Thoreau had that very evening gratified Mrs. Toth by approving her plans to attend a concert at the Albert Hall on the following afternoon.

During the séance itself, Susan had stationed herself in the room adjoining the Spirit Parlour. In this room, there is a ventilator high in the wall which communicates with the parlour. Through it, Susan had fanned into being the breeze that had stirred when I first inquired for the presence of a disembodied spirit. She used a sheet of tin for this purpose, subsequently substituting a bunch of freshly-cut pine boughs obtained through arrangement with a local forester. As Mr. Thoreau himself noted, fragrances powerfully evoke reminiscences, and Susan and I felt the scent of pine was highly reminiscent of the deceased Transcendentalist, who had never been so happy as when treading some lonely forest walk.

This should give a sufficient idea of Susan's utility, Dear Reader. As she helped the Toths with their coats and cloaks, I threw her a smile combined with a rueful shrug. Since she had been in the next room, she already knew about the sitting's premature end and what had caused it. She might have known in any case, as Mrs. Toth was still peeved with her son and taking no pains to disguise it.

"I shall be leaving to visit friends in the country next week, Madame Fox," she told me. "But I would like to schedule another sitting for the twelfth of next month—assuming Absalom has made no alternative arrangement."

She accompanied her words with a pointed look at her son. He cringed in response and ducked his head like a whipped dog. It was an ugly thing to witness, Dear Reader. I endeavoured to catch his eye as he passed through the door, and to smile at him again by way of expressing my sympathies. But since he looked quickly away on meeting my gaze, it seemed my gesture went for nothing.

"They're a queer lot and no mistake," observed Susan, once the door was shut behind them. "Even for Spiritualists, they're queer."

I was forced to agree, Dear Reader. "At any rate, they have good taste in their Spirit," I said. "I've enjoyed reading Henry David Thoreau's writings. They're much superior to the usual scribblings of somebody's featherheaded aunt or half-illiterate son. The man could write—though he had a perverse streak that appears now and then, to be sure."

"Never more than when he was courting Mrs. Toth, I'm thinking," said Susan cheerfully. "Ah, well: I'd best get supper on the table. I don't doubt you're hungry, and I know I am. There's a note from Inspector Harper come for you," she added casually. "A constable brought it around during the sitting."

I stiffened at these words, but forced myself to respond in the same casual manner. "Very well," I said. "Let me change out of these clothes, and I'll see what he wants."

Just then the doorbell rang. Frowning, we both turned to look. "I'll get it," I said. "It's probably just somebody for the dentist next door. You go ahead and see to the supper."

Because we share our building with a dentist, Dear Reader, we often get dental patients who have mistaken our entrance for his. When I opened the door, however, I found not a toothache sufferer but Absalom Toth. His strange pale eyes were fixed on me as he said, "I beg your pardon for disturbing you, Madame Fox. But I believe I left my gloves behind in your Spirit Parlour?"

All unsuspecting, I let him in and accompanied him into the Spirit Parlour.

This room, Dear Reader, is the heart and soul of my business. I have taken pains to make it impressive, with black velvet hangings festooned with braiding and tassels; statues of gods and goddesses on pedestals; and of course the séance table itself on which rests the Electrical Spiritograph. But at the moment, it was too dark to see much of anything, since all the lights were extinguished.

"I'll just light the lamps," I said, "and then we can look for your gloves." As I spoke, I was moving toward the row of alabaster oil-lamps that line the walls of the parlour. They give a much brighter light than the candle-lantern I use during séances.

"Never mind the lamps," said Mr. Toth.

His voice startled me, for he had come up behind me in the dark without my being aware of it. The next moment I found myself locked in his arms, undergoing as determined an attack on my virtue as I have ever experienced. It was not merely a matter of stealing a kiss, Dear Reader. One of his hands groped at my décolletage; the other was endeavouring to work its way beneath my skirts, and all the while he was forcing his tongue into my mouth.

For a moment, surprise held me motionless. He was such a strange, sexless creature that I would never have supposed him capable of such an assault. So as I say, surprise held me paralyzed for a moment, but only for a moment. Fortunately, he had taken my compliance so completely for granted that he had made no effort to guard against any counterattack.

Pulling one hand free, I struck him as hard as I could across the face.

He let go of me at once, his eyes wide and his mouth hanging open. Even in the dark room, the print of my hand was visible against his pallid skin.

"How dare you?" I demanded. "How *dare* you?"

He stared back at me wordlessly, Dear Reader. It was evident that he was astonished by my reaction—astonished even to the point of speechlessness. This made me angrier than ever. "How dare you?" I repeated.

He spoke at last, in a baffled-sounding voice. "I . . . thought you wanted it."

I drew back my hand to strike him again. He shrank away, with the cringing manner he had shown toward his mother. "I thought you wanted it," he repeated. "I'm sorry."

"How *could* you think such a thing?" I demanded. "What encouragement have I ever given you to treat me that way?"

"You smiled at me," he said.

Now it was my mouth that was hanging open, Dear Reader. "Do you imagine any woman who smiles at you is encouraging you to treat her like a strumpet?" I said, as soon as I had recovered enough to speak.

He did not answer, but continued to stare at me with his wide, pale eyes. "I'm sorry," he said again.

"And well you should be," I said. "Get out, now. And if you ever attempt such a thing again, *I shall tell your mother*."

It was a ridiculous threat, Dear Reader, given that Mr. Toth was a full-grown man in his mid-thirties. But it was effective nonetheless. He shrank further. "No! Please don't," he said. "It shan't happen again, I promise."

"It had better not," I said grimly. "Now go."

He went, but with an air of puzzlement, Dear Reader. It was evident he felt his behaviour had been quite rational, and that I was irrational to resent it. It was all I could do not to strike him again.

Chapter 2

I was still fuming over Mr. Toth's behaviour as I changed my clothes. Mixed with my anger, however, was a sense of unease.

I am no virginal innocent, Dear Reader. It is true I have never been married, but though technically a spinster, I have some acquaintance with what are referred to as marital relations. Quite a bit of acquaintance, actually. Growing up in the Spiritualism business, my upbringing was emphatically not a sheltered one. In my long and varied career, there had been more than one man with whom I had enjoyed marital relations without actually undergoing marriage as a preliminary.

Not, I hasten to say, that I ever earned my living by so doing. Spiritualism is my trade, not Prostitution. But I am obliged to admit that all these alliances were contracted at least partly for reasons of expediency, thus blurring the line a bit. Nevertheless, I am as far from embracing Prostitution as its antithesis, Free Love.

This may require a bit of explanation, Dear Reader. In previous memoirs, I have stated that I never had any truck with Free Love. I will clarify that statement here, as one or two Readers have pointed out that the term Free Love is sometimes construed to refer to any extra-marital relationship.

What *I* consider Free Love, as practiced in Spiritualistic circles, has idealism as its basis—though it is an idealism that coincides all too opportunely with male desires. Think of Mr. John Humphrey Noyes and his system of Complex Marriage, in which promiscuous relationships between his followers were encouraged to the point of forbidding exclusive ones. Although a woman might in theory be free to choose congenial partners under this system, in practice she might find herself unable to refuse one, if he happened to be favoured by Mr. Noyes.[5]

My own relationships, in contrast, were not formed for idealistic reasons at all, but rather practical ones. This is not to say that they were not also enjoyable. A sensible woman will always try to kill two birds with one stone, and I am nothing if not sensible. Indeed, I would argue that since most women in our society are dependent upon men for their livelihood, this is not much different from marriage itself, which often has as much a practical as an idealistic basis—or at least one in which practical and idealistic motives are mixed.

That had always been my argument, Dear Reader, and it had satisfied me up till now. But thanks to my evolving relationship with Detective Inspector Thomas Harper of Scotland Yard, I could no longer feel quite so satisfied. I was, in fact, feeling increasingly defensive about my chequered past.

I had become acquainted with Inspector Harper as a result of the Langley affair, which had taken place two years ago.[6] His acquaintance had been thrust upon me then quite against my will.

---

[5] Especially if he happened to *be* Mr. Noyes.—*Ed.*

[6] See *Ghost in the Machine.*

I had always regarded policemen as the natural enemies of Spiritualists. Although our occupation is not forbidden by law like Fortune-Telling, it often falls under the same kind of disapproving scrutiny from those who enforce the law. And not without reason, as I must admit. Although I generally take care to obey the law myself, I regularly employ other people to break it.

These are minor breakages, by and large, committed to obtain the information I need to impress my clients at the séance table. I pay valets and lady's maids to copy their master and mistress's letters; hairdressers and bath attendants to report gossip imparted by clients during moments of relaxation; caretakers and landladies to let my agents into the rooms of the recently deceased to collect material that can be used to my advantage.

Admittedly these are ignoble acts, Dear Reader. But I would argue that the end justifies the means. The end, in this case, was happy clients cheered by the idea that Death is not really the end, but only a stepping-stone to a more sublime existence.

I will not say that I converted Inspector Harper to this point of view, Dear Reader. But he was generally willing to turn a blind eye to my methods, in part because I chose clients who could spare the money they spent in my Spirit Parlour, and partly because my means of obtaining information were often better than his. The police very commonly employ informants and agents whose methods are no more scrupulous than mine. It was, once again, a case of the end justifying the means.

So far, so good; but of late a complicating factor had crept into our relationship. I hesitate to call it Love, Dear Reader. Young lovers have their claim to the world's sympathy, but middle-aged ones are apt to appear merely fatuous—especially when both parties have seen as much of the dark side of Human Nature as the Inspector and I had done. So I will put it rather that the two of us were struggling with a strong mutual attraction whose exact nature and terms we had yet to define.

The struggle had been going on for a good six months now. It centred around the fact that he was conventional enough to prefer marriage as a preliminary, while I was unconventional enough to feel we might dispense with marriage and forge full speed ahead (so to speak).

This is contrary to the usual male/female dynamic, as you will note. More typically it is men who shy away from marriage and women who pursue it. But that is because women typically have more to gain from marriage than I did. I already had a comfortable home; I wasn't interested in having children; and I had a job that enabled me to support myself very well. I was, in fact, making more money than my would-be bridegroom. Under the circumstances, marriage wouldn't benefit me much. It would be more likely to injure me.

That is not to say it would injure me in a financial sense. Thanks to the Married Women's Property Act, I could secure my money for my own exclusive use, even after marriage. Inspector Harper had urged me to do so, thinking no doubt that this formed part of my objections. He knew me well enough to understand that I would want to keep my hard-earned savings in my own hands. But in fact my main objections were personal rather than financial—and so personal that I did not even like to speak of them, for fear of hurting his feelings.

Part of it was his job, Dear Reader. I felt I was already compromising a good deal by allowing him into my heart and home. Policemen are *personae non gratae* in many of the circles I frequent, and that includes high circles as well as low ones. I felt a natural reluctance to compromise any further, especially since I didn't see that it was necessary.

Then, too, the mere idea of marriage had its fearful aspects. As a Spiritualist, I had been in a position to see some beautiful enduring unions that lasted even beyond the death of one of the spouses. But I had seen plenty of the other kind, too. My own parents' had been a case in point: a union that had been a mistake from almost every perspective beyond the undeniable fact that it had produced *me*.

As for Inspector Harper, he had yet more personal reasons to be leery of matrimony. For he had already experienced it firsthand, Dear Reader, in the years before he met me. It had not been so disastrous a union as my parents', as I gathered, but still it was easy to guess from things he said and left unsaid that it had not brought either party a conspicuous degree of happiness. And for this, once again, his job had been to blame.

It is true that his late wife's objections to police work were different from mine. She had objected rather to the long hours, unpredictable absences, and inadequate pay associated with his job. She had also shrunk from the brutal nature of the crimes he was obliged to investigate and which he would have occasionally liked to discuss with her, as a means of easing his mind.

Frankly, none of that was likely to bother *me*. My own work also requires long hours and makes unpredictable calls on my time, besides paying well enough to make a husband's salary immaterial. As for brutal crimes, I certainly do not approve of them, but I found his cases interesting and enjoyed discussing them with him. Sometimes I had even been able to help solve them, and that had been enjoyable, too.

But to marry him—to take the irretrievable step of becoming his legal helpmate and partner? That would be not only a step farther, but a step into the unknown. He might be willing to accommodate me on financial matters, but there would be others on which I would undoubtedly have to accommodate him. It would be foolish to think that marriage would not change my life in some fundamental ways.

And by and large, I was happy with my life as it was. Indeed, not so very long ago, Dear Reader, I would have considered my present existence ideal. I had my charming little Temple with its loyal Spiritualistic clientele; I had a devoted staff of three people to assist me in my work; I had my own horse and carriage and all the other trappings of respectability without the actual burden of being respectable. And thanks to my skillful use of all these assets, I was now what I would once have called rich, though my bank balance didn't seem as impressive as it would have years ago.

In fact, none of it seemed as impressive as it would have years ago. There is an inflation in human hearts, Dear Reader, as in economic matters. Even knowing I was well off, I yearned for more. And most of all I yearned for him: the man he was, the pleasure I found in his company, and the greater pleasure our ripening acquaintance seemed to promise. I just wasn't yearning for marriage.

Knowing that he was yearning, too, you might have supposed we could reach a compromise. We ourselves had supposed as much some months earlier, and it had been amusing at first to argue matters back and forth: for him to try to carry his point and me mine. But of late it had been not so much amusing as frustrating. And the frustration had reached a boiling point just the previous evening.

We had come back to the Temple late, after a recherché little supper at the Grand Café Royal. Under the stimulus of a couple of brandy-and-sodas, and the knowledge that all the servants were out of the house, he had been encouraged to kiss me. One thing had led to another, and things had gone rather far between us—rather far, I say, but no farther. He was a man of iron self-control, as I had reason to lament.

It occurred to me that it might be interesting to see how far his self-control extended, purely in the spirit of scientific inquiry.

"*What* do you think you're doing?" he had inquired, in a strangled voice.

I reminded him that he was a detective and urged him to use his powers of deduction. Whereupon he had sworn at me and then left, rather abruptly.

Naturally I had not taken this well, Dear Reader. It felt like a fling at my scarlet past. His own past was, in contrast, quite stainless. He had never made love to any woman besides his late wife. And it was clear that he did not propose to make love to me, unless and until he married me—assuming he still wanted to. I tended to doubt that now, for what had happened that evening had been not only a rebuke, but a rejection of a very personal sort.

I don't take rejection any better than most people—not as well as most, I daresay. After he left, I did a good bit of swearing myself. I told myself I wanted nothing more to do with Detective Inspector Thomas Harper.

Clearly he was an ungrateful wretch, lacking in address as well as common sense.

He had left me hurt and angry and in a state of inflammation that extended to both body and soul.

I told myself that nothing he had to offer could possibly be worth compromising my hard-won independence. Indeed, it was quite possible that his reticence in bedroom affairs was only to cover up some inadequacy. Even if I desired to marry him, it would be prudent to ascertain this point beforehand—not to buy a pig in a poke, as it were.

I told myself that there were plenty of men in London who would be glad to indulge me in my perfectly natural desires without demanding that I marry them first. I had woken up that morning assuring myself that I would be much better off finding one.

And then Absalom Toth had tried to force himself upon me. Under the circumstances, it seemed something more than a coincidence.

The incident would have been funny, Dear Reader, if it had not been so horrible. I felt I would rather be celibate all my life than let Mr. Toth touch me again. Even as it was, I had the urge to scrub my lips and arms and bosom—every part of me he had touched—with strong carbolic soap. The mere thought of allowing him further intimacy made my mind shy away in horror.

It was very inconvenient that it should be so. From a purely practical point of view, it would have been a solution to a vexing problem—essentially a problem of supply and demand (to put it in economic terms once more). But I wanted no part of such a solution, Dear Reader. That was very clear to me now. I could not even contemplate an affair with some other, more appealing man. It was Inspector Harper whom I wanted, or no one.

And I could not help worrying that he might no longer want me.

I could not help worrying, likewise, that I had somehow been responsible for what had happened this evening. The idea that simply smiling at Mr. Toth could have prompted an attempted rape seemed incredible. I wondered uneasily if my state of mind or body might have been perceptible to him through some animal sense, encouraging him to think me willing.

At least he could not think it any longer, which was some comfort. But it left me in a nasty position all the same. I would be forced to look at his pale, unwholesome face every week at the séance table, unless I was willing to sacrifice one of my best clients. I didn't think I was willing to go that far, but I couldn't honestly look forward to our next meeting.

As I unlaced my corset, combed out my fox-coloured hair, and wrapped myself in my dressing gown, I wondered what Inspector Harper would think of the incident. After the unfortunate way we had parted the previous evening, perhaps he would not care. He might even feel I deserved it. Likely I would never know, as I had not heard a word from him since.

And then I recalled that Susan had spoken of a letter that had come during my sitting. Knotting the belt of my dressing gown, I hurried downstairs.

"You took long enough," commented Susan as I entered the Sitting Room. Then, looking at me narrowly, she asked, "Has something happened?"

I had been of two minds whether to tell her and Jenny about Mr. Toth. Normally I tell Susan and Jenny everything—at least everything pertaining to my business. Susan, as I mentioned before, has been with me for over a decade and has proved herself more than worthy of trust. Jenny has only been with me a little less than two years (not coincidentally, the same period I have known Inspector Harper), but the circumstances of our relationship have likewise inspired a strong mutual trust.[7] Looking at their faces, I suddenly resolved to tell them all about it.

I had expected they would be shocked to hear of Mr. Toth's behaviour. But they listened with a composure that amazed me. It amazed me, at least, until I learned the reason for it. "Is that all?" said Susan, with a shrug. "He tried to kiss *me* a while back."

"Me, too," said Jenny.

"This was more than a kiss," I said sharply.

"Same kind of business, though," said Susan. "You see it a lot when you're in service. Doesn't matter how respectable you look or act. Gentlemen of his sort always think it won't hurt to try. If you poker up and take offense, they just pass it off as a joke."

---

[7] See *Ghost in the Machine*

This ought to have made me feel better, Dear Reader. Clearly Mr. Toth's behaviour had been prompted by nothing specific to me. But in fact, I felt affronted in a whole new way. I had been assuming that whatever his motivation, it must have included *some* personal element—that he had, at the very least, found me attractive.

To learn he had found Susan and Jenny equally worthy of his attentions was rather dampening. Susan, as I have noted, is staid and middle-aged in appearance, while Jenny, though much younger, is red of face, strapping of build, and more wholesome-looking than beautiful. I am not beautiful, either, but I take pains with my appearance and am accustomed to hear myself described as a well-looking woman. It irked me to find myself lumped together in their company.

"Why did you tell me nothing of this before?" I demanded.

Again Susan shrugged. "Not worth mentioning. As I say, you get used to it in service. Since I was holding the card-tray at the time, I just whacked him over the head with that, and he never tried it again."

I switched my attention to Jenny. Owing to some painful incidents in her past, she has a very low tolerance for gentlemanly misdemeanours. Not only that, but she is big enough and strong enough to enforce her displeasure. "What did *you* do?" I asked, with some curiosity.

"Boxed his ears," she said briefly.[8]

[8] Readers should not confuse this with the kind of ear-boxing that takes place in "The Adventure of the Cardboard Box," as detailed by Dr. John H. Watson. In this context, boxing someone's ears merely means that they slapped them.—*Ed.*

"Good for you," I exclaimed. "I did the same thing, though probably not as effectively."

She shook her head, looking grim. "I wouldn't have thought he'd try such a thing on a lady like you," she said. "Maybe I'd better have a word with Sam about him."

Sam is her husband and my coachman—a hulking figure of a man. I have no doubt he could flatten Absalom Toth into the ground with the greatest of ease. "It's tempting," I told her. "But I don't think Mr. Toth will try such a thing again. I said I'd tell his mother if he did."

"Seems to me you'd do better to tell Inspector Harper," said Susan, eyeing me a little curiously.

Fortunately, Jenny spoke up before I was obliged to make any reply. "That reminds me," she said, producing an envelope. "That's from him right there. It came during your sitting. A constable brought it around."

I nodded, and as soon as Susan had served us with soup and veal-and-ham pie, I picked up the letter and broke the seal. I felt considerable anxiety in doing so, but the letter's opening lines reassured me:

> *Dearest Seraphina:*
> *I hope you will forgive my unceremonious departure last night. I have been regretting ever since both the words I spoke then and the impression I may have given (quite inaccurately) that I was in any way displeased with you. Please be assured that nothing could be further from the truth.*

There followed a few more lines, expanding on this idea in a flattering way. The letter concluded:

> *I hope you will allow me to tender my apology in person at your earliest convenience. Awaiting word from you, I am,*
> *Yours in Spirit and so forth,*
> *Thos. Harper*

All this was written in even lines in his best handwriting, as though wrought with great care. But there was also a hastily scrawled postscript:

> *Seraphina, there has been a development in a recent police case that seems to have some connection with you and your affairs. I hope you will allow me to call upon you tomorrow to discuss this development, as well as the matter mentioned above—T.H.*

I looked up from this missive to encounter Susan's eye. "Good news?" she asked.

"I hardly know," I said. Gratifying though the body of the letter might be, I could not help feeling a bit anxious at the prospect of being embroiled in another police case.

Still, I reminded myself that it might not be anything important. And there was undoubtedly cause for rejoicing in knowing the Inspector had not been offended by my forwardness the previous evening. "On the whole I think it *is* good news," I said. "I shall take it as such, at any rate. Let me send a note round to him, and then we can open a bottle of champagne to celebrate."

Chapter 3

We had our champagne, which I thoroughly enjoyed now my greatest worry had been set to rest. After a glass or two, I was even able to see the lighter side of my encounter with Mr. Toth.

"Only think of him fancying I would welcome his advances," I said with a shudder. "I cannot imagine any woman doing so."

Susan, refilling her glass, opined that he was a gormless fool whom one might pity under other circumstances. "His mother has him properly under her thumb," she said. "Anyone can see that."

"And trying to force himself on other women might be his way of compensating," I agreed. "But I'd as soon not think about that any longer. It rather turns my stomach. Have we any new business?"

"There's a whole lot of papers come from that Italian woman who was here the other day," said Susan. "She said you was wanting them."

"Oh, yes," I said, sitting up with interest. "Signora Mazzara. Let's see what she has sent us."

Signora Mazzara was a new client, Dear Reader, and one whose business was a refreshing change from my usual Spiritualistic endeavours. The signora was a celebrated opera singer who had recently suffered a humiliating setback in her career. Seeking for a way to recover from it, she had decided to commission a new opera from the same librettist whose work had originally launched her on her career years before.

Unfortunately, Signor Russo had died before completing his new libretto. Signora Mazzara had at first been devastated by this second setback, but then it had occurred to that there might still be a way to complete it, via Spiritualism.

Such a commission was, as I say, a refreshing change from my usual business. It seemed likely also to be a feather in my cap, socially speaking. Opera is Art with a capital "A" and very fashionable among London's elite classes. Helping to complete Signor Russo's unfinished opera might bring me some very nice publicity, of the kind most likely to do me good. I said as much to Susan and Jenny as I opened the package containing the late librettist's papers.

"But do you really think you can write an opera?" asked Jenny anxiously.

"I don't have to write the music," I explained. "Only the libretto—the story on which the opera is based." I had made sure of this point before accepting the commission, Dear Reader, for my musical accomplishments are not extensive. I can shake a tambourine, or strike a few plangent chords on a guitar in a dark room, but little more.

"But do you think you can do it?" persisted Jenny.

"I don't see why not," I said. "The plot's the least important part of an opera, as far as I can tell. Indeed, if you look at the plots of some of the most famous ones, they're complete nonsense." I had already done this myself, Dear Reader, and been much encouraged. "Besides, this libretto's already half-written. If we look at what Signor Russo left behind, we ought to be able to deduce enough to finish it off after some fashion."

"I wonder the signora didn't think to do that herself," commented Susan.

"Oh, she's rather simple in some ways, though shrewd enough in others." I gestured toward the stack of papers in front of me. "Imagine her being credulous enough to simply give me all this! Ordinarily I'd have to pay some agent to sneak into Signor Russo's rooms and steal it for me. But I told her I needed all his personal papers in order to concentrate his Spirit Energy here at the Temple, and she fell for it completely. I wish my job were always this easy!"

It soon developed, however, that my exulting had been slightly premature. "My God," said Susan, laying down a sheet of paper with a stunned expression. "I never saw such a handwriting. If it *is* handwriting, and not some kind of cypher."

"And of the bits I *can* read, none of them look as though they have anything to do with opera," I lamented. "This, for instance, is clearly a laundry list. And this appears to be a half-finished letter to his mistress."

"Named Arthur?" said Susan, who had been inspecting the letter meanwhile.

I snatched it back from her and subjected it to a closer scrutiny. The name did appear to be Arthur. "Well, it's not for us to judge," I said. "But perhaps it's as well Signora Mazzara didn't go through these papers herself! She seemed to think Signor Russo cherished a long-standing passion for *her*. Though I did rather gather it was a passion of a more cerebral than physical sort."

We found a few other things of interest amid that heap of papers, Dear Reader, but precious little dealing with any unfinished opera. "It was to be called *Night and Day*," I said. "That seems pretty clear. And the plot seems to involve some sort of conflict between what he calls the Man of Light—or it might be *Men* of Light—and the Woman or Women of Darkness. But I'm damned if I can make out any more than that." I shoved the heap of papers away from me with a disgruntled sniff. "And I was told the thing was half-finished! Why, it's hardly begun, by the look of it."

"Perhaps the signora wasn't so credulous after all," said Susan, grinning. "Maybe she took *you* in, not the other way around."

"That's as may be," I said coldly. Pushing back my chair from the table, I announced that it was late, and that I for one was tired. "I vote we postpone any further discussion of the subject until tomorrow."

***

A good night's sleep did much to restore my optimism, Dear Reader. The idea that I would be meeting Inspector Harper later that day also helped put me in a buoyant mood. Compared to some of my commissions, this one seemed unlikely to pose any great difficulty. I had looked at the plots of enough operas to feel certain I could cobble together something that would be, at the very least, no worse than the usual jumble of improbabilities.

"But the plot isn't all of it, is it?" said Susan. "Isn't the librettist supposed to write the words of the songs, too?"

I told her I had no doubt I could manage that part of it also. "Mere doggerel verse—that's all most of it is. It doesn't even have to rhyme. The music is the important part."

"Who will write that?" Jenny wanted to know.

"Mr. Percival Witters. He's probably the best-known British opera composer there is, though I must confess I'd never heard of him until I took this commission. But the signora said he's been involved in the project from the beginning."

"Then maybe he knows the plot already," said Susan. "Which might be inconvenient if your version doesn't agree with his!"

I told her I was prepared for this eventuality. "He's going to be at the séance, so I intend to sound him out beforehand, to get an idea of how much he might know. And of course, it takes a while to spell out answers with the Spiritograph. So I can be alert to developments and adapt as we go along."

"Is anyone else going to be there?" asked Jenny. "Besides the signora and Mr. Witters?"

"Mr. Alfred Hinney, the manager of the opera house. Naturally *he'd* want to be there, for he's the one who's paying for all this."

Jenny looked puzzled. "I thought it was the signora's idea," she said. "That she wanted this new opera to help her career."

"Yes, but it's Mr. Hinney who's paying for it. I wish it weren't so, for his being there makes me nervous. The others are artistic types and likely easy enough to fool, but he's got the reputation of being a hard-headed businessman."

Susan was looking a bit dubious. "And you still want to do that extra business at the beginning of the séance?" she said. "With the rose and music box?"

"Yes, I do," I said. "I don't see that it's much of a risk, there at the beginning. But of course, we'll have to stay on our toes. If it looks like there's going to be trouble, I'll just say the Spirit Energy isn't working and call the whole thing off. But I confess I'd be disappointed if I had to do that. I've never had anything to do with opera before, and I've got some original ideas for this one, if I do say so myself."

***

Our first sitting with the signora was to take place that evening. As if that were not excitement enough for one day, I had also Inspector Harper's visit to look forward to. I had written that I would receive him at four o'clock that afternoon. So when the doorbell rang at exactly four, I withdrew to the Sitting Room, pinned a welcoming smile on my face, and arranged myself on the sofa (the scene of our late contretemps, as I could not help remembering).

My welcoming smile slipped a bit when Susan ushered him into the room. For he was not alone, but accompanied by another man: a big, blond, good-looking gentleman with a flourishing moustache.

"Madame Fox," said the man, sweeping off his hat and bowing. There was an assurance in his manner that, while not exactly offensive, was still unexpected, considering that he was a stranger to me. I looked at Inspector Harper for enlightenment.

His eyes met mine with an air of apology, Dear Reader. He has grey eyes, keen and intelligent and often alight with humour, but they seemed more weary than humourous today. His whole manner seemed a trifle weary, in fact. Or perhaps it was merely that he was standing beside the other man, who was very much younger than he was. In any case, I found myself noticing the lines on his face and the grey in his hair more than I usually did, as he took my hand and bowed over it.

"I do beg your pardon," he said in a low voice. "Beg it twice over, in fact. I had intended to come alone." In a louder voice, and with a sideways look at his companion, he added, "The circumstances I alluded to in my note have unfortunately taken on a new urgency. This is my colleague, Detective Inspector Freemantle."

"Pleased to make your acquaintance, ma'am," said Inspector Freemantle, bowing again with the same air of brisk assurance.

I was not surprised to hear he was a policeman, Dear Reader. Under the circumstances, it was only to be expected. But it did surprise me that he was a detective inspector. He seemed rather young to have achieved promotion so soon. "Is this regarding some case?" I asked, as soon as the introductions were complete and both men had taken seats at my bidding.

Inspector Harper opened his mouth to speak, but his colleague got there first. "Oh, yes," he said. "You've probably heard that we've had a series of murders involving . . . women of a certain type." He primmed up his mouth as he spoke, with evident distaste. "What you might call Woman Unfortunates."

I *had* heard of the murders he was alluding to, Dear Reader. All London had heard of them by now, though the first few had gone almost unnoticed. Crimes of violence against women of this sort are so common that it had taken three or four of the poor creatures getting killed before some bright spark at Scotland Yard had put two and two together and realized there might be a connection.

"But what connection could those murders have with me?" I asked, looking from one man to the other.

This time Inspector Harper got there first. "This latest victim," he said, "Matilda Bird, the one who was killed over in Bermondsey near the docks. She had one of your cards in her possession."

This rocked me back on my heels a bit, Dear Reader. Again I looked from one man to the other. "Matilda Bird," I repeated.

"Was she one of your customers, ma'am?" asked Inspector Freemantle eagerly.

"Clients," I corrected, just as Inspector Harper also spoke. "Clients," he told his colleague. "The preferred term is clients."

Our eyes met briefly, in a moment of shared amusement. When I looked again at Inspector Freemantle, I found he was surveying us both with a speculative expression.

"Clients, then," he said. "Was Matilda Bird one of your clients?"

"No," I said with certainty. Then, with rather less certainty, I added, "At least not under that name."

"I suppose she *might* have used an assumed name to come here," said Inspector Harper, looking at his colleague. "Have you the photograph, Ned?"

The younger man produced a folding case, opened it, and took out a photograph. He made as if to hand it to me, but Inspector Harper stopped him. "It was taken after death," he explained. "You might find it . . . unpleasant."

"Ought to have warned you," agreed Inspector Freemantle, with an air of chagrin. "Beg your pardon, ma'am."

"The doctor cleaned her up as well as he could," went on Inspector Harper. "But it's still not pleasant."

"Her throat was cut," said Inspector Freemantle matter-of-factly. "Very nasty business. Perhaps you ought to call your maid to bring you some smelling salts, in case you come over faint?"

I said I thought we could dispense with that precaution, whereupon he handed me the photograph. I took it rather gingerly, Dear Reader, but in fact it wasn't too bad. The young woman's eyes were closed as if she were sleeping, and there weren't any marks of violence on her face. There was an unpleasant suggestion of sutures about the neck, to be sure, but I had been prepared for worse.

I gave the pictured face a long and searching scrutiny. "I don't believe I have ever seen her before," I said. "Certainly she has never been one of my clients."

Both men looked disappointed. "You're sure about that, ma'am?" said Inspector Freemantle.

"Quite sure," I said, handing him back the photograph. "I wonder how she came to have my card?"

"Oh, that might be accounted for easily enough," he said. "I suppose you hand them out by way of advertisement and post them in the shops and so forth. Probably a lot of them floating about."

I opened my mouth to contradict him, Dear Reader, for in fact I do not advertise in this wholesale way. My business is a very exclusive one. But then it occurred to me that to say so might focus police attention on me again, just when I was likely to be rid of it. So I closed my mouth and said nothing. I saw Inspector Harper's eyes rest on me thoughtfully, as if he guessed I was keeping something back. He is difficult to deceive in that respect.

But in fact I had no wish to deceive *him*. I had every intention of telling him the truth, once we were alone together. It was only his colleague in whom I was reluctant to confide. This was the more so because he was now speaking of the murdered woman in a way that irritated me, though it was clearly meant to flatter.

"It's not likely you'd have had any dealings with such a woman anyway, ma'am," he told me. "By all accounts, she was a very low sort—no better than she ought to be, as the saying goes."

"Indeed," I said, regarding him coolly. "I don't suppose she would have elected to earn her living in such a way, if she had had any choice."

With a tolerant smile, Inspector Freemantle advised me not to listen to the cant of well-meaning reformers. "She might have earned her living in a hundred respectable ways," he said. "Or she might have married, which is the properest occupation for a woman anyway."

This statement irritated me yet further. "You forget that marriage is not an occupation she could choose for herself," I said sharply. "Our society reserves to men the right of choosing, not women. And you may have heard that there's a shortage of marriageable men in this country just now. That means there are some hundreds of thousands of what the newspapers are pleased to call 'superfluous women.' And even if a woman *is* able to marry, that doesn't mean her difficulties are over. What if her husband abuses or abandons her? What if she has children to support?"

Faced with these home questions, Inspector Freemantle threw a harassed look at his colleague, as though expecting him to intercede. Inspector Harper merely sat with his arms folded over his chest, however, and regarded us both with an expression grave and impassive.

"And it's not as though any of the higher professions were open to Miss Bird," I went on. "Men do their best to keep medicine and law and the church all within their own exclusive domain, even to women who can obtain the necessary education. Which I doubt was the case with *her*."

"Well, she wasn't alone in that," said Inspector Freemantle. With another look at Inspector Harper, he added, "There's a lot of us men, too, who had to scramble into what little learning we could, the best way we could. Nothing more than a few years of grammar school, and sometimes not even that. Unlike my colleague, here, with his Eton and Oxford education."

I sensed that this was a long-standing grievance between them, Dear Reader. But I did not let it distract me from my point. "Nonetheless, even without a university education, you have had opportunities no woman would have," I told him. "I have yet to learn that Scotland Yard employs my sex in any but the most menial capacities. What response do you think Miss Bird would have met with, had she applied for the position *you* hold?"

"Still, she might have kept herself respectable," argued Inspector Freemantle. "Thousands do."

"Yes, and thousands more die trying," I retorted. "Would you expect her to earn her living as a beggar? Or a match-girl? Or to make artificial flowers in a garret for pennies a week, so she might starve in a genteel way? Likely prostitution seemed her only real choice."

Inspector Freemantle's mouth was now drawn into a stubborn line. "It's very charitable of you to take that view, ma'am," he said, "very charitable and Christian. But I've seen a lot of women of that sort, and I can tell you that they don't deserve your sympathy. Thieving, pox-ridden creatures given over to every kind of vice."

"If they do have pox, it's likely because some man gave it to them," I said instantly.

"Having first got it from a woman of the same sort!"

"But I doubt it was given him *forcibly,*" I said. "Likely he would have had more choice than the woman in the case, at any rate."

Inspector Freemantle summoned up a laugh. "Well," he said, "I can see you feel strongly on the subject, ma'am."

"I do," I said. "And pox is hardly the worst danger such women face. Only look at these murders you are investigating. How many have there been now—four? Five?"

It was Inspector Harper who answered my question. "We think five," he said. "But there's some question about this latest murder at Bermondsey. It doesn't seem to follow quite the same pattern."

"Ah, but you know my theory about that," said Inspector Freemantle, with all his assurance now restored. "It's some madman with a religious monomania. Just look at the locations where all the crimes took place. *Cross* and Crown, *Church* Street, White*chapel*, *Worship* Street: there's a religious theme in all of them. *And* they've all taken place during the dark of the moon. It's well known that the moon exerts a strong influence on lunatics."

"I thought it was the full moon that was supposed to incite lunacy," I remarked.

Inspector Freemantle looked irritated at my putting my oar in again, Dear Reader. But he responded civilly enough: "Ah, there's no use expecting a madman to go by hard-and-fast rules, ma'am. And of course, the dark of the moon would make it easier for him to conceal his crimes."

"But then he would be acting from motives of expediency, not lunacy," I pointed out, "which doesn't seem consistent with his being a madman at all."

With an air of crushing all argument, the inspector said he had consulted a well-known alienist, who had quite agreed with his theory. If he thought this would impress me, Dear Reader, he was wrong. You would scarcely believe the foolish theories propounded by well-known alienists.[9] Before I could make this point, however, Inspector Harper intervened.

"At any rate, there doesn't seem to be a connection with this place," he observed. "We'll have to mark that lead off the list, Ned."

Inspector Freemantle agreed that they would. Having thanked me for my help, he resumed his hat, looking quite ready to go. "I suppose it's time we got back to the Yard," he said. "Are you coming, Tom?"

"You go on ahead," said Inspector Harper. "I must just have a word with Madame Fox first."

---

[9] Madame Fox may be alluding here to the work of Dr. Sigmund Freud, who had already achieved a considerable reputation by the date of this writing (c. 1882). Admittedly, however, he had not yet promulgated some of his more egregious theories (i.e., penis envy).—*Ed.*

Chapter 4

After his colleague had left, Inspector Harper turned to me and made as though to speak. I shook my head at him, however. "Just a moment," I said.

The Sitting Room door was standing ajar. I went over and found (as expected) that Susan was standing behind it with a notepad and a pencil. "That will do," I told her. "I don't need notes for *this* conversation."

She eyed me rather satirically as she responded, "Very well, ma'am. I'll just go put the kettle on for tea, shall I?"

"Do," I said. "I'll ring when I want it." And I shut the door in her face.

Inspector Harper had watched this exchange with amusement. "So you keep up your old practice of making transcripts, do you?" he said. "No conversation goes unrecorded?"

"It's come in useful once or twice," I said. "As you might remember." I gestured toward the Sitting Room sofa. "Sit down, Tom. That is, if you dare to remain, now your chaperon's gone."

He coloured quite charmingly, Dear Reader. "You know I'm sorry about that business the other night," he said, as he seated himself on the sofa. "Deuced sorry. And if I wanted a chaperon, I would find a more agreeable one than Ned Freemantle!"

"Rather a bumptious fellow," I agreed.

The Inspector ran a hand through his hair. "*I* find him so," he said. "But there's no denying he's got a lot of energy."

"Largely misplaced, by the sound of it."

"I *would* agree with you," he said, "except it might be accounted jealousy. There's no denying he's risen quickly in the force. Far more quickly than I, in fact."

"And without the advantage of a university education, too," I added mischievously.

With a rueful shake of his head, the Inspector said he failed to see that it was much of an advantage. "Ned's always going on and on about it, but honestly, it's hard to see why. As I say, he's risen faster than I have. And he's likely to rise farther, too. One of our chief inspectors is retiring soon, leaving a vacancy in the rank just above ours. It wouldn't surprise me to see the job go to him over me—university education notwithstanding."

I told him I hoped it would go to the better man instead. "And I mean better in every sense, Tom, not just in education. You are his superior in wit, charm, and intelligence—and good looks, too, of course—"

Smiling, he reached out to draw me down beside him. "Ah, now that sets me up in my own esteem! I think most women would consider Ned a good-looking man."

I conceded that Inspector Freemantle was good-looking, but said his manners did not recommend him to me. "*Or* his opinions, either. But we need not discuss him any longer, I hope."

He agreed that we need not. "I wouldn't have brought him here today, but he rather forced my hand. Your card being found at the murder site, you know, and he the investigating officer. Before that happened, I had meant to come alone. To apologize." His eyes met mine very squarely and sincerely. "I am sorry about the other night. What I said then—you must forgive me, Seraphina. I was rather . . . overwrought, you might say." He smiled with some embarrassment. "I'm not entirely certain *what* I said, only that I did not behave with much gallantry."

Assuming a reminiscent air, I said that he had, among other things, called me a heartless temptress, which at my age might be counted a compliment. He assured me he had meant it that way, on the whole. "At least the temptress part, not the heartless," he said. "I know you've got a heart. You wouldn't mean to hurt me."

"No," I said, looking at him with astonishment. "Whatever I was meaning to do, it was not to *hurt* you. Quite the contrary, in fact."

"Yes, I know," he said. Once again, his colour had risen. "I don't mean hurt *that* way."

"What do you mean, then?" I asked.

He looked down at our joined hands. "I've told you before," he said, "that when I was younger, I was a bit of an idealist. My family wasn't what you'd call rich, but I was given a good education and expected to pursue some respectable profession. Law was indicated, as I had a barrister uncle who was willing to take me into partnership. But any respectable profession would have done."

"And instead, you chose to join the force," I said, having heard this story before. "Quite against your family's wishes. Because you thought it was work worth doing."

"Yes," he said. "And I still think so, by and large. But you can't do police work for long and stay much of an idealist. It's not only the crimes themselves, but the way they're prosecuted—the inequity in the system, and the fact that you're a part of it. For a man with ideals, it's sometimes hard to swallow."

I nodded again, and he continued, "One way and another, you rationalize it. You argue it's the system that's corrupt, not you. That you yourself are a man of honour." He looked at me with a touch of humour. "Can't you see why I might hesitate to take a step that most people would consider highly dishonourable? There isn't much that I *haven't* compromised on over the years, but I've never compromised on that."

Put that way, I could see it, Dear Reader. Of course it was very inconvenient—as inconvenient as my own squeamishness in regard to Mr. Toth. But the Inspector's ideals were a part of him, and a part that I rather admired when they did not conflict with my own desires.

"Well," I said, as lightly as I could, "you certainly weren't compromising the other night!"

He shook his head, his expression still humourous. "Ah, you don't know what a near thing that was," he said. "Between you and me, you came within a hair's breadth of having your way with me. I don't say my behaviour was heroic in itself, but under the circumstances it was certainly self-sacrificing. And I'd argue that's at least one of the elements of heroism."

I agreed, though forbearing to say it was a heroism not altogether to my taste. He divined my thought, however. "You still don't understand," he said. "Feeling as we do about each other, I might agree that there was nothing wrong in giving way to our feelings. But if you'd spent as much time in the police courts as I have, you'd hesitate to put any woman in a position where she'd be liable to a charge of criminal intercourse. That's what they call it, you know," he said, holding my eyes with his own. "Criminal intercourse. And I've seen more than one case where a woman's life was completely destroyed, after her private affairs were made public."

"Oh," I said blankly. That was a hard objection to counter, Dear Reader. Even if I had never been charged with criminal intercourse before, that didn't mean it couldn't happen. Likely those other women had thought it couldn't happen, either. I might argue that I was clever enough and discreet enough to take the risk, but I couldn't deny that there *was* a risk, or that the risk increased with each repetition. As Susan is wont to say, the pitcher goes to the well once too often.

"Oh," I said again. "Well, I can see why you might favour marriage, then, under those circumstances."

"And I have a better idea why you are against it," he said, "after hearing you argue with my colleague." After a moment's pause, he added, "I hope you know I would never beat you, or abandon you."

"I do know it," I assured him. "I only mentioned those things to make my point generally, Tom. And because he irritated me so much."

He seemed cheered by this statement. "In any case, it would be a brave man who tried to beat *you*," he said. "Even in argument! I'm guessing Ned will think twice before trying it again."

This idea seemed to cheer him also. The next few minutes were taken up in a purely personal exchange, which established beyond doubt that our relationship was restored to its former happy footing. It was some minutes more before I recalled that I had a confession to make.

"A confession?" he repeated. "That sounds rather ominous."

I could guess what he was thinking and hastened to reassure him. "It's nothing very shocking," I said. "Not a *personal* confession at all. It's merely something I did not like to say in front of your colleague. The fact is, his assumption was incorrect."

"What assumption do you mean?"

"The assumption that there are a lot of my cards floating about. In fact, I don't hand them out to anybody who isn't a client or likely to become one. And that's a pretty restricted field."

He frowned as he considered this information. "I see," he said. "So Miss Bird having your card would indicate there might be a connection between her and one of your clients?"

"It seems the obvious conclusion," I said unhappily.

I could guess what was coming next, and it did, quite predictably. "Could you give me a list of your clients?" he asked.

I told him I did not like to do that. "It's a matter of confidentiality, Tom. My position is like a clergyman's in that respect. I hear some very private confidences in the course of my work, which I feel obligated to keep private. And there's the business aspect of it, too. Most of my clients are people of high standing—or at least think they are. They wouldn't take kindly to being linked with a series of brutal murders involving women of low reputation."

"I understand that," he said, "but if there *is* a link, I would hope you'd want to establish it. Especially considering how eloquently you were speaking just now of the plight of the victims."

That is the devil of eloquence for eloquence's sake, Dear Reader. Having taken such a position, I was obliged to live up to it, or be diminished in his eyes. He and Jenny were always doing this to me—acting as a kind of external conscience, when my internal one would have been perfectly happy to lie quiescent. At this rate, I am likely to become a reformed character in short order.

"Perhaps we could compromise," I said, after a moment's thought. "If you could give me more information about the crimes and the evidence you've found, I could see if it indicated some specific client. At the very least, it might help narrow the field down."

It was his turn to think. "Yes, I could do that," he said. "In fact, it might be a good idea anyway. A woman's perspective is often useful, especially in crimes of this sort."

"Sex crimes?"

"Surprisingly, they don't seem to *be* sex crimes. You'd assume they were, given the occupation of the victims. And a lot of the newspapers have jumped to that conclusion. But according to all the medical men who've examined the bodies, there was no 'connection,' as they put it, between the murderer and his victims."

I was surprised to hear this, Dear Reader—surprised and rather relieved. It was some comfort to know the poor creatures hadn't been violated as well as murdered. "Maybe it *is* a religious maniac," I said.

He smiled wryly. "It's possible. Ned is pretty strong on the theory, as you may have gathered. But it seems to me it could equally well be coincidence that the murders have all occurred near places that have some religious association. I mean to say, if you look around London, you'd be hard put to find a place that *isn't* near some church, or former nunnery, or a street that's named for a saint."

I agreed that this was so. "Have the murders anything else in common?"

"Only the profession of the victims. They were all Unfortunates—women who'd engaged in prostitution at least intermittently. But apart from that, they're a pretty disparate lot. Two were married; two were single; one was a widow. One was very young—not out of her teens. Miss Bird, on the other hand, was in her thirties, and the other three considerably older."

"I gathered they all met their death in the same manner, however?"

He nodded. "Yes, their throats were cut. And it was done the same way in each case—by someone standing behind them. What's more, none of the victims appears to have made any resistance. Our theory is that the murderer approached them as a potential customer and negotiated for a—er—rearward approach." His eyes met mine briefly, and with some embarrassment.

"I suppose that might conduce to the theory of a religious maniac," I said, keeping my voice determinedly matter-of-fact. "He wanted to make sure they *were* prostitutes, before executing judgment upon them."

Inspector Harper agreed this was possible. "But as I say, I think the circumstances could be explained equally well by a common or garden maniac—someone who simply enjoys killing women and chooses the ones who pose the least risk to him. It's a sad fact, but when a prostitute is murdered, it doesn't elicit the same public outrage as a victim from a more respectable walk of life."

We talked the matter over a bit more, focusing especially on the character of Matilda Bird. "Was she the one who was killed in the street?" I asked, trying to recall the various newspaper accounts I had read of the murders.

"No, Molly Barlow and Effie Jones were both killed in the street. Ellen Pierre's body was found in the foyer of a building, while Kate Little was found under a bridge. But Miss Bird was killed in her—well, not her room exactly, for she didn't live there. It was rather a room which she rented for—how can I put it? —professional purposes."

"And that's where my card was found?" I asked. It was a curious thought, Dear Reader: my card serving as a witness to a murder.

"Yes," he said. "I gather it was amongst some books and papers that were also found there. I wasn't one of the officers who investigated the scene, but I read the report afterwards and volunteered to approach you, since I already knew you." He smiled and squeezed my hand. "Knew you pretty well, too—well enough to know Ned Freemantle wouldn't get any change out of you if he came by himself!"

I agreed this was likely enough. "But you haven't seen the room yourself?"

"No, just the reports and sketches and so forth. As I say, I wasn't among the officers who investigated the scene." He looked at me with sudden interest. "But I'd like to see it. And perhaps you might like to see it, too? There might be something in the room that would suggest a possible line of investigation to you, which wouldn't appear in the written accounts."

I said I would like to see the room very much, Dear Reader. It might be a ghoulish curiosity, but I thought it was a natural one, seeing that the place might bear some connection with one of my clients.

As we were making arrangements to visit the room on the morrow, there was a scratching at the Sitting Room door. After a brief pause, such as might allow a couple in the throes of passion to put themselves in decent order, Susan put her head inside the room to say that the kettle was about boiled dry. "*Do* you want any tea?" she asked. "For if you don't have it soon, you won't be getting any—at least, not before your sitting."

A glance at the clock showed me this was true. "Bring the tea by all means," I told her. "And the Inspector will stay for a cup, too, I hope."

He was glad to do so, saying he had had no time for lunch, and that he had been obliged to forgo breakfast as well because his landlady had failed to get the food on the table in time for him to eat it. I have conceived a deep antipathy for this woman, Dear Reader, sight unseen. If you accept a policeman as a lodger, you ought also to accept that his hours will be irregular, and that his mealtimes might need to be put forward or backward to suit his needs. But Mrs. McIntyre seemed to regard all such requests as personal insults, and to take a malicious pleasure in thwarting them.

"She ought to make you a reduction in your board, considering how often you are obliged to miss meals," I said indignantly. "It's bad enough you have to forgo sleep for days on end when an important case is in hand, without being deprived of food, too."

He seemed amused by my indignation. "Mrs. McIntyre is far from being the worst of her kind," he said. "If you'd seen some of the boarding places I've tried—unaired sheets, unswept floors, bad drains, and so forth—you'd be glad to settle for missing an occasional meal. Especially when you can have the shortage made up so pleasantly." He looked with approval at the tea-tray that Susan had just brought in.

This appeased me, of course. I helped him to tea and sandwiches, and while we ate the conversation turned to my own affairs, specifically to the séance that evening. He had heard about the signora's commission and agreed it sounded interesting. "But do you really think you can write an opera?" he asked, echoing Jenny's skepticism. "Even if it's just the libretto, it seems to me you might have promised more than you can deliver."

"O ye of little faith," I said. "I'll have you know that I have been in close communication with the Spirit of Roberto Russo for the past few days. And together we have come up with some splendid notions."

He smiled as he drank off his tea. "No doubt you'll deliver the goods, then," he said. More soberly, he added, "At any rate, there doesn't seem much danger in your trying. Not like some of your past commissions."

"Yes," I agreed. "It's hard to see how I could get into trouble writing an opera!"

Chapter 5

That evening, as I welcomed Signora Mazzara, Mr. Witters, and Mr. Hinney into the Temple of Spiritualism, I looked them all over with interest.

I had already met Paola Mazzara during our initial interview, but a second inspection confirmed my first impression. She might have been divinely fashioned to appear on a stage. Everything about her was a little larger than life: big dark eyes, a wide mouth set with dazzling white teeth, and a figure you could not mistake for anything but feminine even from the topmost row of the gallery. She had also a charming accent and regal air which gave credence to the generally accepted idea that she was of noble Sicilian birth, though I knew from my own private investigations that she had really been born in the East End of immigrant parents and was thus a native Londoner.

Percival Witters, the composer, was also of striking appearance. His dark hair was streaked with white and stood up on his head like a dandelion gone to seed. He had a clean-shaven face with a disproportionate amount of forehead and an expression of godlike disapprobation. The disapprobation seemed particularly strong whenever he looked at me. When the signora had introduced us, he had scowled, nodded, and looked away as if my features pained him. Now he stood glaring down at my Sitting Room rug as though that pained him, too.

Mr. Hinney, the manager of the opera house, seemed by contrast perfectly willing to be pleased. A big, genial bear of a man with a bushy black beard, he had enveloped my hand in his on being introduced and said how glad he was to make my acquaintance. "This is quite the venture of Paola's, isn't it?" he said, with an indulgent look toward the signora. "She's a very determined woman, Madame Fox. There's no gainsaying her. Why, even poor Russo dying isn't going to stop her from staging this opera!"

These words brought Mr. Witters's attention up from the rug. "There would be no reason not to stage the opera in any case," he said sharply. "I would have been quite capable of writing libretto as well as music—quite capable. I have done so many times before. My genius is a complete one."

"Of course it is, Percy," agreed Mr. Hinney, with the air of humouring a small child. He winked at me as he added, "We all know you're a complete genius. But this is Paola's little venture, and there seems no harm in trying it her way."

The signora, meanwhile, had made a dismissive noise. "I have read the libretti *you* have written," she informed Mr. Witters, "and I tell you frankly I prefer Roberto's. I have no objection to your writing the music, however."

"And I have no objection to writing the music, either," he returned, "assuming you can sing it."

The signora's eyes narrowed. "*What* do you mean?"

"Only that your last *Lucia* at La Scala was, by all accounts, a complete disaster."

The signora swore volubly in Italian and English. It was an impressive performance, Dear Reader. "That was the veriest fluke," she cried. "I tell you I had been tried to the utmost that day. The claques, the petty persecutions—you can have no idea."

"Yes, yes, Paola," said Mr. Hinney, patting her arm in a soothing manner. "We all know it was a fluke. And the best way to prove it is to finish this new opera with Madame Fox's help and show everybody that your voice is as good as ever."

As he spoke, his eyes met mine. There was a clear suggestion in their depths that it might be as well to get on with things, seeing that the children were growing fractious. I nodded, then announced, "I can feel the Spirit Energy gathering around us. It is time we began."

We proceeded into the Spirit Parlour, where I arranged the party around the table. I put the signora at my right, Mr. Witters at my left, and Mr. Hinney across from me.

As I took my own place at the table, I saw Mr. Hinney glance around the room with appreciation. He had the air of admiring a well-crafted stage set. Of course that was pretty much what it was, Dear Reader. I found myself warming to him more every minute. He might not be a True Believer, but it was clear he had no intention of causing trouble.

The signora, too, looked likely to cause no trouble. She sat with her head thrown back and her face drawn into an expression of religious ecstasy. One might have supposed she was the Medium, not I.

Mr. Witters I wasn't so sure about. The look of disapprobation was still strong on his face, but he had taken his place at the table obediently enough and placed his hands as I had shown him, fingers outstretched so that our little fingers just touched. Normally we hold hands at séances, but there are times when this alternate posture works better for one reason or another. I had a particular reason for choosing it this evening, Dear Reader: one of my hands was not a real one. It was my right hand, whose little finger was just touching the signora's. It looked the same as the other—black-gloved and ornamented with rings—but in fact it was a dummy, leaving my real right hand free underneath the table.

"Is there a disembodied spirit in the room?" I intoned.

Mr. Hinney and Mr. Witters looked around at these words, and the signora straightened up and opened her eyes with an air of pleased expectancy. I could feel the little breeze that Susan, standing behind the ventilator in the next room, had stirred into being. For the next business, she had something more to do than stir breezes. I was careful to wait a good minute before repeating the question.

"Is there a disembodied spirit in the room?"

In answer came a few low tinkling notes, weirdly dislocated in the dark room. "Ah," cried the signora, whipping her head around to identify their source. Mr. Hinney smiled. Once again, he had the air of admiring a clever piece of stagecraft. Mr. Witters, however, scowled at the sound of the tune. This was only to be expected, as it was not a tune he had written. It was in fact an aria from Signor Russo's first opera. Although he had written only the lyrics, not the music, I had thought it an appropriate motif nonetheless.

We had had a music box specially commissioned to play this tune, Dear Reader. Concealed by the Japanese screen, Susan had crept through a door in the wainscoting and wound it up. It was the sort of thing that was often done at séances years ago. I had thought it a nice touch for this one, given its musical theme.

"Is there a disembodied spirit in the room?"

At this third inquiry, the Spiritograph chimed. This naturally caused the three clients to focus their attention upon it. And while their attention was so focused, a full-blown rose appeared seemingly out of nowhere and landed in front of the signora.

She gave a startled cry. "Roberto?" she asked, staring at the rose with wide eyes.

The bell rang again. "Ah, Roberto," she cried. She seized the rose in both hands and carried it to her lips. "Roberto, *caro mio!*"

This gave me the opportunity to slide my dummy hand off the table, secrete it in a pocket in my skirt, and put my real right hand on the table in its place. I had worn a dress with wide sleeves, so it was easy enough to make the substitution without being noticed. It had been equally easy to conceal the rose inside my sleeve and flip it out onto the table with my right hand while everyone's attention was distracted. It had been many years since I had dealt in Apports—objects appearing from the Spirit World—but I was pleased to see I had not lost my touch.

The signora, meanwhile, was laughing and crying and explaining to the room at large how *cher* Roberto had gone without food so he might present her with roses after every performance when they were youngsters just embarking on their operatic careers. She had told me the same story at our initial meeting, which was where I had gotten the idea in the first place.

"We grew up together, you understand, and opera was to us both the breath of life. My first leading rôle was in *his* first work, and through it we both achieved fame. No one has understood me—my soul—my *art*—so profoundly before or since. He was my first love, and my greatest," she said, rolling her eyes dramatically.

I reflected that her Roberto seemed to have taken a slightly different direction in his subsequent loves, but naturally kept my reflections to myself. After the signora had finished rhapsodizing, I got down to business. Having inquired if the Spirit present was that of Roberto Russo, purely as a formality, I continued: "Signor Russo, we are gathered this evening to finish your last opera, which you were unable to complete on this Earthly Sphere."

The wheel on the Spiritograph began to rotate. "N-I-G-H-T A-N-D D-A-Y," it spelled.

"*Night and Day,*" agreed the signora eagerly. "Yes, yes, that was its name." Mr. Witters and Mr. Hinney both nodded.

So far we were in agreement. I ventured another statement. "The opera treats of the meeting of the Man of Light and the Woman of Darkness."

The bell rang.

"The Woman of Darkness," repeated Mr. Witters in a meditative voice. "*And* the Man of Light. A metaphor for the struggle between good and evil. Not original, of course, but yes, it has possibilities." His eyes kindled as he went on: "The Woman of Darkness is a figure we see again and again in art and literature. The Dark Lady—Queen of the Night—a wicked heart concealed beneath a veneer of beauty, tempting Man from the path of virtue."

This wasn't at all the direction *I* had contemplated for the opera, Dear Reader. If nothing else, it sounded completely hackneyed, casting the woman as scapegoat as usual. Hastily I spelled out on the wheel: "Woman of Darkness not evil but rather keeper of hidden knowledge."

No wheel had a chance against Mr. Witters, however. He didn't even notice it moving. "The Man of Light is initially tempted by the Woman of Darkness," he explained to us all. "But though he initially succumbs to her wiles, his instincts warn him of danger."

I rang the bell imperatively—not in agreement, but just to get his attention. He swept on regardless. "And in the end, he vanquishes her. She sings a last great aria of defiance and fury."

The signora looked interested but a little dubious. "A death scene, yes," she said, as if tasting the idea. "I excel in my death scenes, certainly."

"And the Man of Light triumphs, alone."

"No," I said sharply. "No, he doesn't."

They all looked at me in astonishment. "He doesn't," I repeated. "That's not how the opera goes at all."

Mr. Witters looked affronted, the signora surprised, and Mr. Hinney amused. "How does it go, then?" demanded Mr. Witters.

"Wait," I said, pushing back my chair. The Spiritograph obviously wasn't going to work with this group. "I shall summon Signor Russo directly and let him speak through my lips."

I fetched in the late signor's papers—to serve as a focus for his Spirit, as I explained. I brought in the sherry decanter as well. It struck me we might also need a little of the lubrication provided by that sort of Spirit. Mr. Hinney asked if he might have a whiskey-and-soda instead, so I rang for Jenny to bring in a tray with a whole array of Spirits. Having swallowed a goodly measure of sherry by way of inspiration, I laid my hands on the papers.

"The Man of Light is the leader of the Men of Light," I announced, "just as the Woman of Darkness is the leader of her Women."

Everyone nodded. Mr. Hinney's eyes twinkled at me over his whiskey-and-soda. "The Men of Light believe the Women of Darkness are evil," I went on, "but in fact they are wise and virtuous. They possess a deeper knowledge—a knowledge instinctive and intuitive, which has been lost to the Men of Light."

Mr. Witters, looking mutinous, opened his mouth to dispute. I raised my voice and went on. "The Women were forced into the Darkness generations ago by the ancestors of the Men of Light. The present-day Men believe it was done because the Women were evil. But it was really done to deprive them of their rightful inheritance. Their rightful inheritance in the—er—Light. You," I said, turning a compelling look upon the signora, "you, as their leader, know this truth. But the Man of Light is genuinely convinced his people acted from motives of virtue. Thus, when he encounters you, he is fearful and prepared to strike you down."

The signora nodded, her expression that of a resolute leader prepared to defend her people at any cost. I, meanwhile, was improvising rapidly, not having fully evolved this part of the story. "But he doesn't strike you down because—because another threat suddenly arises. A horrible creature that threatens you both."

"A dragon," said Mr. Witters at once. The signora flashed him a look of admiration.

"*Si,* a dragon," she agreed.

I would have been willing to accept a dragon, Dear Reader, but Mr. Hinney observed that dragons had been done quite a bit, what with one thing and another. We bent our thoughts to another alternative. "Goblins?" I suggested, thinking of Miss Rosetti's poem.[10] "Goblins in grey—twilight figures between Light and Dark—symbolizing deception and false knowledge."

Everyone liked this idea. "Let's have a Goblin King, too," suggested Mr. Hinney. "Basso part—make a good rôle for old Bert Cutworth. I always like to send a bit of business his way when I can," he explained to me in an aside.

"Basso aria—set in D minor," said Mr. Witters. He had got out a notebook and was making notes as we spoke. Glancing up with a look of irritation, he asked me if we couldn't have more light in the room. I got up and lit all the lamps, reflecting that this was a séance like no other.

Having reseated myself at the table, I went on with my narrative. "So the Goblin King arises while the Man of Light is threatening the Woman of Darkness," I said.

"And the Man of Light turns from her to vanquish the Goblin King, thus saving her from this threat and earning her love and gratitude," finished Mr. Witters, nodding.

"No," I said. "*She* saves *him.*"

The signora looked surprised at this and Mr. Witters taken aback. Even Mr. Hinney looked a little dubious. "Generally it's the

---

[10] "*The Goblin Market.*"

hero who saves the heroine," he told me. "There's Leonora,[11] of course, and a few others, but generally it's the hero who saves the heroine unless the plot demands it."

"The plot does demand it. That's how the Man of Light knows he can *trust* the Woman of Darkness—because she saves his life," I explained. "And once he knows he can trust her, her beauty quickly conquers him."

The signora cast down her eyes with a modest smile.

"And so he is willing to listen, and to learn how he and the other Men have been deceived. But the other Men of Light aren't willing to listen—at least, some of them are, but there's one who isn't. He's the Man of Light's second-in-command, and he urges them to fight the Women."

"Baritone rôle," said Mr. Witters, scribbling away. "Duet with hero, first and second acts. Solo aria."

"And all the Women aren't happy about the idea of reconciling with the Men, either. You," I said, addressing the signora, "have a faithful advisor and counselor among the Women who urges against trusting any Man."

She nodded vigorously.

"The two sides make preparations for battle. Their leaders urge them against it, while their seconds argue for it. At the last moment, the Goblins appear in force, and both sides must turn to conquer this common threat. And so they are reconciled."

"But the Man of Light is fatally wounded in the conflict," said Mr. Witters, kindling into enthusiasm once more. "Carrying out the idea of star-crossed lovers whose love is doomed from

[11] Heroine of *Fidelio*, Beethoven's only opera.—*Ed.*

the start. The Woman of Darkness sings a wrenching aria of pain and love over his dead body. Or perhaps his dying body. We might make it a duet then, and—"

"No," I said. "It's his former friend and rival who is killed. The Man of Light and the Woman of Darkness go on to—er—live happily ever after."

Mr. Witters shook his head stubbornly. "A tragic ending is more artistic," he said.

"*Si*," agreed the signora, nodding vigorously once more.

"But audiences like happy ones," said Mr. Hinney. He smiled at me. "Yes, it's got possibilities. But there are a few details I'd like settled before we go any further."

The sherry and whiskey sank low in their decanters while we discussed the details. We agreed calling the characters by their titles was cumbersome. Clearly, they needed names. Mr. Witters suggested calling the Man of Light Lucien, derived from the Latin for light. I saw no harm in letting him have his way on this point, and indeed, it gave me the idea of suggesting Melanie as his counterpart's name, derived from the Greek word for darkness. I was pleased to have this suggestion approved, but less pleased to have the hero's friend and rival dubbed Apollo. Still, it was appropriate enough, and I reasoned Mr. Witters deserved a few concessions.

"And we also need a name for Melanie's friend and advisor," he went on.

"Susan," I said, without thinking.

Mr. Witters shook his head and said Susan was a pedestrian name. I glanced apologetically toward the ventilator. "Egeria would be much more suitable," he told me, "conveying the meaning of an advisor or companion." And Egeria it was, rather to my discontent.

Still, I had my way in other things. For the opening scene, Mr. Witters envisaged the Men of Light arriving on a ship and disembarking on the shores of the Women's land. "Not a ship but an *airship*," I said. "Much more up-to-date."

"Nonsense! You couldn't land an airship on a stage," said Mr. Witters scathingly.

"I don't know about that," said Mr. Hinney. He rubbed his bearded chin reflectively. "I daresay we might rig something up, to give the idea of an airship flying in. And it'd be a real draw to audiences. A very original notion," he added, looking at me approvingly.

I was indebted to dear Monsieur Verne for the notion, Dear Reader, but did not say so. We sketched out the details of the first act: an opening chorus sung by the Men of Light, followed by a duet between Lucien and Apollo: "Fear the Night." Lucien, abjuring this advice, would then wander off alone to explore and get caught by nightfall, giving him the opportunity to express his fear in a tenor aria.

At this point Melanie would make her entrance, bearing her Staff of Power. She would lay it aside in order to pick some night-blooming flowers, accompanying this business with a song, "Night Sets Her Foot." I invented some very pretty lyrics for this, Dear Reader, which won even Mr. Witters's approval, though I will admit a lot of them came verbatim from Henry David Thoreau's journals.

Having foolishly laid aside her staff to croon over flowers, Melanie then found herself weaponless when Lucien sprang out to confront her. At this critical juncture, the Goblin King would appear and threaten Lucien in song, only to be driven offstage by Melanie, who had meantime retrieved her staff. She and Lucien would then sing a melting duet, "Is This My Enemy?" The song would end with the two embracing, this part of the business witnessed by Apollo, who would go on to sing an aria of disillusionment at seeing his leader consorting with the enemy.

"And very nice, too," was Mr. Hinney's approving comment.

The second act would open with a chorus performed by the Women entitled "Moonlight." "Transformation scene and procession," said Mr. Witters, scratching away with his pencil. "And I suppose you want a ballet." He threw a disparaging look at Mr. Hinney.

"Audiences like 'em," said Mr. Hinney apologetically. "You know that as well as I do, Percy."

Following the ballet would come a duet between Melanie and Egeria, the latter urging Melanie to caution. "Laying the ground for her treachery later on," said Mr. Witters, nodding. "We'll have her an older woman—"

"Yes," said the signora firmly. "*Much* older."

"—and that means she must be a contralto."

I looked at him coldly, Dear Reader. It happens that my own voice tends toward the contralto. "Susan—I mean Egeria—isn't treacherous," I said. "Just cautious. A bit *overly* cautious, perhaps." Again I glanced toward the ventilator.

"She has to be treacherous," said Mr. Witters, as one explaining a basic fact of life to an ignoramus. "Just as she has to be a contralto. It's a dramatic convention."

"Then let us defy it. Make Apollo the treacherous one."

Mr. Hinney said he thought there was a pretty sound dramatic tradition of treacherous male seconds, too, and for his part he liked my idea. He did not speak one word for every fifty spoken by the others, Dear Reader, but what he did say was admirably shrewd and to the point.

Following her duet with Susan/Egeria, Melanie would meet Lucien again by prearrangement. He would express his uncertainty about embracing both her and the wisdom she offered, which would inspire her to sing the climactic piece of the whole opera: "Do You Not Dream?" I had come up with some pretty good lyrics for this, too: "Night has a thousand stars, where day has only one," which was soundly scientific as well as poetic, and "Close your eyes, love, and see with the eyes of the mind," which would convey the Women's innate quality of intuition.

"Yes," said the signora enthusiastically. "Yes, yes, yes. And the aria shall culminate with an A over high C."

Mr. Hinney looked dubious, and Mr. Witters downright skeptical. "That's where you came to grief as Lucia, wasn't it?" he said.

This produced another furious outpouring of profanity in English and Italian. "You think I cannot do it?" she demanded. "You think I cannot? I will show you, you filthy pig—son of a dog—*maledetto bastardo!"* And flinging back her head, she let loose a staggering volume of sound in a nearly inhuman key.

The Spiritograph chimed softly. I did not operate the switch, Dear Reader; it rang all by itself. I looked at it uneasily. The Signora, however, indicated it with a triumphant smile. "You see? Roberto, *he* knows." Directing her attention again to Mr. Witters, she ordered, "You will write me this aria, and I will sing it, to great acclaim."

He accepted this dictum meekly, Dear Reader. We went on to settle the details that followed: Apollo's decision to betray his leader, and his further, fatal decision to enlist the Goblins' aid because he thought them enemies of the Women. "But in fact the Goblins are *everyone's* enemies," I explained. "The first thing they do when the battle begins is to turn on their own ally and slay him."

This action would be preceded by brief scenes in both camps as they prepared for battle, and then the battle scene itself. Apollo's death would follow: the usual kind of drawn-out operatic business that would allow him to express his remorse in a duet with Lucien ("Now I Know the Dark Indeed"), undergo a change of heart, and urge a reconciliation with the Women before expiring in his friend's arms. "I see Nino Adriano as Apollo," said Mr. Hinney. "Just his kind of rôle. And what would you say to Benjamin Cardle as Lucien?"

The signora, after a moment's consideration, agreed that Mr. Cardle was *molto simpatico*. Mr. Witters said dryly that in his opinion Mr. Cardle wasn't entirely sound in the middle registers, but that he supposed he could take that into consideration when he was writing the part.

With Apollo and the Goblins disposed of, the opera would then proceed smoothly to its end. Melanie and Lucien would sing their joyful vision of a future in which Dark and Light might have equal share and honour, and then the whole cast of Men and Women would come together in a final triumphant chorus, "To the Stars," as Melanie and Lucien sailed away together in the airship.

"Not *my* idea of opera," said Mr. Witters sourly. "A lot of new-fangled nonsense, as far as I'm concerned. I'd as soon see the old traditions kept up."

"Of course you would, Percy," said Mr. Hinney. He spoke sympathetically, but there was a suggestion of a twinkle in his eyes as he added, "Still, the old traditions were new once, you know. One has to keep up with the times or be left behind altogether."

Altogether, it was one of the more interesting séances I had ever staged, Dear Reader. Undoubtedly it was one of the longest. Susan was yawning as she helped the clients with their coats and showed them to the door. She was inclined to be short with me, perhaps because of fatigue, but I thought the Egeria business might have played a rôle, too. I reckoned I would have to handle her with kid gloves for a day or two until she got over it.

Chapter 6

Owing to the late hour I had gone to bed, and the quantity of sherry I had imbibed, I wasn't feeling quite my usual self when I arose the next morning. But a cup of coffee helped dispel the mental fog, and on the whole I was very pleased with the way the sitting had gone.

"I never saw such a business," was Susan's disapproving comment. "Not a séance at all if you ask *me*. Just talking and talking until I thought you'd never be done. And even at that, it didn't sound as though you got the business half settled."

"No, but my part is mostly done," I said. "And between you and me, I might easily leave the rest to Mr. Witters if I wanted to. But I plan to keep my hand in, helping out with the dialogue and finishing up the song lyrics. They liked the ones I gave them last night."

In this, Dear Reader, I was counting on being able to draw further on Mr. Thoreau for inspiration. He is so unknown in this country that I reckoned I was safe from any charge of plagiarism—especially since I could always claim I had gotten his Spirit's communications confused with Signor Russo's. Being a Medium is a great advantage in that respect. It wasn't as though I were claiming they were my *own* verses.

"And we might as well not have bothered with that music box," was Susan's next discouraging comment. "All a needless expense, and it's not as though we're likely to use it again."

"No, but it went over very well," I said. "You managed that part of the business splendidly." I hoped this compliment would please her, but it only reminded her of another grievance.

"That's as may be, but I've told you before I'm too old to scramble around on my hands and knees in the dark. That door in the wainscoting is hardly big enough for me to squeeze through."

"That's so it will be inconspicuous," I said. "But I daresay we might have it enlarged a trifle, if it's really inconveniencing you."

Susan pulled down the corners of her mouth and said it would be just more needless expense. "It's not like we use that door much anyway."

"No," I agreed, "but it's convenient to have it when we need it."

Jenny, who had been listening to this exchange, now asked what the opera was about. I told her—at some length, Dear Reader. "A lot of nonsense, if you ask *me*," added Susan, with a sniff. "Goblins and airships and I don't know what else."

"Will you get to see the finished opera?" Jenny wanted to know.

"Yes, indeed," I said. "Mr. Hinney has promised me my own box for opening night. And I'm to attend some of the rehearsals as well. I think he's hoping I'll be a counterbalance to Mr. Witters, who's inclined to be rather hidebound in his notions." Glancing at Susan, I added, "The idea that of any two women, one must be treacherous! I hope you appreciate the way I saved your character."

"*My* character, is it?" said Susan. "Then if that Melanie character's meant to be you, all I can say is that she's being played by someone who's got as good opinion of herself as *you* do. *And* a regular Billingsgate jaw."[12]

There was clearly no conciliating her as yet. I gave it up for the time being and went to get ready for my outing with Inspector Harper. A visit to a murder scene hardly constitutes a pleasure outing, but I was still looking forward to spending some time in his company. As I supposed we might encounter other policemen, I dressed myself in quiet street clothes—dark dress, mantle, and veiled hat—and was waiting when he arrived.

***

I was wrong about there being other policemen at the scene. The Inspector explained that the police had finished their investigation some days previously. There wasn't even a constable on duty when we arrived. A few curiosity-seekers were still gathered on the pavement, gazing up at the place with open mouths and avid eyes, but the great London mob had obviously moved on to later and larger sensations.

The place looked like an ordinary lodging house from the outside: three stories of soot-stained brick and shabby enough to pass unnoticed in that quarter. Inside, it was still shabby, but in a more flamboyant style. There was a felted paper on the walls, a

---

[12] The vendors of Billingsgate Fish Market were so famous for profane and abusive language that these qualities eventually came to be defined simply by the word Billingsgate.—*Ed.*

parlour full of red plush furniture, and a nude female figure holding a torch that served as the newel post of the staircase.

As we stood looking around at these features, a stout middle–aged woman came bustling out of the parlour. "I can give you the first-floor front if you can wait a bit," she informed us briskly. "Ten shillings and very nice indeed. Or I have a few rooms on the second floor available now. Not so fine as the other, but the sheets are nice and clean, and it's only three shillings the hour."

The Inspector's colour had risen slightly. "We do not wish to rent a room," he told her, determinedly not meeting my eye. "The two of us are here to look at the room where Miss Matilda Bird was killed." He showed her his warrant.

She glanced at it, then at him, with an expression of distaste. "Police again," she exclaimed. "I thought you was all done with that room."

"We have received new information and wish to take another look. We are hoping this lady may be able to shed some light on a clue that was found there."

The woman's eyes went to me then, full of suspicion. I thought I detected alarm as well as suspicion in their depths, but whichever it was, my veil seemed to frustrate her. "Very well," she snapped. "Upstairs, second floor, first door to the right." As we mounted the stairs, she called after us, "You're doing my business no good at all, you know. Matty getting killed here was none of *my* doing. It's not fair I should suffer for it."

Inspector Harper turned to address her sternly. "Renting premises for immoral purposes is against the law," he said, "as you very well know, Mrs. Henley. You've been warned about it before. Several times before, in fact."

The woman compressed her lips. "Yes, and I'll tell you what *I* said before: I only rent the rooms. If people do immoral things in them, I can't be held responsible." With which words, she stepped back into the parlour and slammed the door shut behind her.

With the idea of easing an awkward situation, I asked the Inspector if the woman were well acquainted with Miss Bird, seeing that she had referred to her as Matty.

"Yes, so it seems," he said, "though more in the way of business than friendship. It would appear that Miss Bird was better off than many women of her sort and was able to afford rooms in a lodging house quite decent by local standards. But the very fact of its being decent meant her landlady wouldn't hear of her using the place for immoral purposes. So like a lot of her less fortunate sisters, she'd either make shift to entertain her customers in the street, or she'd bring them here when she had one who was willing to pay the extra cost."

"Here" was a room about ten feet square, dreary as to aspect, but still better than I would have expected, Dear Reader. There was a washstand with the usual vessels, a couple of chairs, a bookstand, and a white-iron double bed-frame with no mattress on it. I thought I could guess why the mattress was missing and averted my eyes with a shudder. This brought my attention to the ceiling.

"Ah," I said, gazing up at my mirrored reflection. Inspector Harper met my gaze in the mirror, then looked away again, his colour rising once more.

It was an embarrassing situation, Dear Reader. It grew even more embarrassing a moment later, when it became obvious that the room next to ours was occupied by a couple engaged in amorous play. Both the Inspector and I immediately began to talk loudly in an effort to drown them out.

"Did anyone see—?" I began.

"I wonder if—" he began.

We both stopped short, whereupon the noises next door became audible again. The Inspector, with determination, began to talk about the crime. "According to Mrs. Henley's account, Miss Bird arrived alone, around seven o'clock P.M. She paid for the room, mentioning that she would like to keep it all night, but that she wanted no supper brought in. Apparently, it was more typical for her to have food brought in around eleven o'clock when she engaged the room for the night. It's quite a usual arrangement, and the servants are accustomed to fetch food from a neighbouring inn."

"I see," I said. "So nobody saw the murderer arrive?"

"It seems not. But how can you tell, with such people? They might lie to save themselves, or because they'd been bribed, or simply on principle because the police were involved."

"If Miss Bird was in the habit of coming here, perhaps they could at least describe some of her usual customers?"

He smiled dourly. "Surprisingly not. Such descriptions as we've been able to get haven't been the least bit helpful. 'Looked like a gentleman—dressed quiet-like. No, can't describe his clothes—just that they were quiet-like. Didn't think he was tall, but not short, either. Couldn't say if he were dark or fair. Couldn't even say if there'd been more than one gentleman, or the same gentleman more than once.' Seemingly they were all too busy to pay attention."

"Most unsatisfactory," I remarked.

"That's why I was hoping you might be able to help," he said. "Your card being found here is about the best clue we've got."

"Where in the room was it found?" I asked, casting a curious look around. "You mentioned, I think, that it was among some books or papers?"

There were only a few books in the room, Dear Reader. This was hardly surprising given the room's usual purpose, and indeed, it seemed to me more surprising that there were any. When I went over and picked one up, however, the reason for its presence became clear. It was an *illustrated* book—the illustrations being not merely suggestive, but explicit.

"Oh," I said, letting it slip though my fingers in surprise. It fell open on the floor, exposing a particularly explicit plate.

The Inspector, colouring, stooped to pick it up. "Yes," he said. "I understand your card was inside one of these books."

"Inside a book of *pornography*?"

I could hardly believe it, Dear Reader. I took the book from him and put it back on the shelf, glancing at the others as I did so. They all seemed pretty much the same: large quarto volumes full of racy illustrations. There was one smaller volume beside them, however, bound in brown cloth. I picked it up, expecting it to be pornography, too, but it wasn't. On the spine were the words *Walden; or, Life in the Woods.*

Chapter 7

For a moment, Dear Reader, I could not believe my eyes. Of all books to find in that room, keeping company with volumes of pornography, *Walden* was the last I would have expected.

I stared down at it as my mind took in the implications. The Inspector, seeing my attitude, came forward and looked curiously at the book in my hands.

"What is it?" he asked.

I showed him the frontispiece.

"Pornography?" he asked.

"Certainly not!"

I rapped out the words sharply, which was unfair to the poor Inspector, of course. His assumption was only natural under the circumstances. Still, I found myself resenting it. As a Medium, one tends to have proprietary feelings about one's Spirits. I felt I knew Mr. Thoreau pretty well after speaking for him these past three or four years, and certainly I was familiar with his books and essays and journals. There was nothing remotely pornographic in any of them. Quite the contrary, in fact. The subject of human sexual relations seemed to have caused him so much discomfort that he could hardly bear to refer to them at all, let alone indulge in them.

But I thought I could guess who might have left his book here, and how my card had come to be in it.

The Inspector was looking from me to the book in puzzlement. "If it's not pornography, what is it?" he asked.

"Philosophy," I said. "Of a very pure and idealistic sort."

His eyebrows rose. "An odd thing to find here."

"Yes, it is," I agreed. I was thinking as I spoke, trying to decide what to do. Part of me—the mercenary part—pleaded against the idea of telling him about Absalom Toth. To do so would endanger my relationship with Mrs. Toth, which in turn would endanger a portion of my income. But on this occasion, I had no trouble getting the better of my mercenary instincts. After Mr. Toth's behaviour the other night, I had been uncomfortable enough with the idea of seeing him again. If he were a murderer, I wanted no further part of him.

The Inspector had been watching my face. "This means something to you," he said. "This book being here."

"Yes, it does," I said. Seating myself in one of the chairs and indicating he should take the other, I proceeded to tell him about the Toths.

He listened carefully, making a note or two, but when I came to the part about Mr. Toth's assault on me, he stopped writing and looked at me with consternation.

"You should have told me," he said. "Good God! Considering the relations in which we stand to each other—"

"At the time, I wasn't sure *what* relations we stood to each other, Tom. You had walked out on me the previous evening, if you will recall. I didn't get your note till later that night."

He looked so stricken that I was sorry I had alluded to the subject, Dear Reader. I went on, striving for a lighter tone. "And when I did get your note, I was so pleased that the other matter slipped my mind entirely. Especially since Susan and Jenny were inclined to make light of it."

He shook his head. "You should have told me," he repeated. "It would have been my privilege to protect you against that kind of thing."

"I was able to protect myself," I said, "as were Susan and Jenny. But I did think about telling you. Only it seemed as though it might be making too much of the matter. I didn't think Mr. Toth was dangerous so much as misguided."

Again the Inspector shook his head. "If it's he who's responsible for these murders, he's very dangerous indeed."

I knew this must be true, Dear Reader, yet my mind boggled at the idea of Absalom Toth as a murderer. It had been hard enough to envision him as a would-be Don Juan. I told the Inspector this, describing Mr. Toth's weedy build and how quickly his aggression had vanished when I had turned on him. "I doubt whether he would have the strength or determination to carry out such brutal crimes."

"It doesn't take much strength to cut someone's throat," returned the Inspector. "Especially if you've taken care to have your victim facing away from you. A woman could do it, even."

I had to concede him this, but another objection soon occurred to me. "Even if Mr. Toth makes a practice of trying to force himself on women, it doesn't necessary link him to these murders. For you said yourself they weren't sex crimes."

"It's true that the murderer hadn't had sexual relations with the victims," he agreed, "but for all we know, the kind of attack he made on you might be simply a feint. Not a true attempt at seduction, but merely a way to manoeuvre you into a vulnerable position and then kill you."

This was a very nasty thought indeed, Dear Reader. If I had shown myself receptive to Mr. Toth's advances, would he have cut my throat? But it seemed unlikely. To kill me in my own Spirit Parlour, with my servants still about and on an evening when he was known to have been on the premises, would have been an act of madness. "I can't believe it," I said aloud. "He would be a lunatic indeed to take such a risk. And not a religious lunatic, either. For I live on Wimpole Street, and I can't see any religious connection with that."

"But you call your place of business a temple," pointed out the Inspector.

This, too, I had to concede, but I soon perceived another objection. "But it wasn't the dark of the moon that night," I said. "And all these murders have been committed during the dark of the moon."

He smiled. "True," he said. "To my mind, that's a more valid objection than the other. As I said before, I doubt there's any religious element to these crimes. That's merely Ned Freemantle's theory, and he hasn't convinced me yet there's anything in it." His expression became pensive. "Though it does sound as though these Toths of yours have some kind of religious obsession." He looked down at *Walden* again.

"Not so much a religion as a philosophy," I said. "Unless you count Spiritualism as a religion, of course. But the Toths eschew all connection with the established church, just as Mr. Thoreau did."

The Inspector nodded. "At any rate, we'll have to look into Mr. Toth's movements on the night of Matilda Bird's murder. In fact, we'll have to do more than that. His book being found at the scene definitely makes him a person of interest, and the police will want to question him."

I had been prepared for this, Dear Reader, but that didn't make me any happier about it. "I'm only assuming it's his book," I told the Inspector. "There's always the chance it might be coincidence."

"But not if your card was found here, too," he said. "And you say Thoreau's work isn't much known in this country. Those two things together seem to put it beyond the scope of coincidence."

It seemed that way to me, too. I watched in depressed silence as he wrapped *Walden* carefully in his handkerchief and put it away in his pocket. "Do you want to look around some more?" he asked. "Or have you seen all you wish to see?"

I felt I had seen everything there was to see, but was glad for an excuse to prolong our outing. I poked about some more among the books, looked out the window at an uninspiring view of roof-tops and dust-bins, and inspected the pictures on the walls.

The pictures were similar in subject to the engravings in the books, Dear Reader. They had been hung at eye level in the upper plastered area of the walls, with the lower part covered by a paneled wainscoting much like that in my Spirit Parlour. This resemblance gave me the idea of looking to see if there might be a hidden door here, too. I found no door, but there were a lot of knotholes in the paneling. When I examined them closely, I discovered something curious.

"Tom," I said, "look at this."

I pointed to a knothole on the wall nearest the bed. He came over to look at it and saw at once what had caught my attention. "It looks as though it's been drilled out with an auger and then plugged," he said.

Leaning forward, he placed his finger on the centre of the knothole and pressed. It gave way, revealing a hole about an inch in diameter. We heard the sound of the plug hitting the floor in the room next door. It was not the room in which we had heard the amorous couple (now mercifully silent), but the one opposite. The Inspector stooped to look through the hole he had just made.

"I don't see anyone there. It looks like an empty room. Very curious."

"Possibly coincidental," I suggested.

He threw me an amused look. "A bit too coincidental for *my* taste," he said. "Right here on a level with the bed, in a room used by couples for immoral purposes. You don't need to have a policeman's mind to guess what's been going on."

"Someone has been watching," I agreed. I looked again at the hole and its proximity to the bed. "But that means someone might have been watching on the night of the murder! Someone might even have seen the murder committed."

"Yes," he agreed. "It would seem so. There's at least a chance." His expression grew resolute. "Mrs. Henley would know if the room next door was habitually used for spying on this one. She *must* know. At the very least, she would know if it were rented the night of the murder and who rented it."

"Then you have another line to follow," I said. "Besides Mr. Toth."

I was very pleased about this, Dear Reader. And I was equally pleased that I had been the one to discover it. Aloud, I observed that it was remiss of Inspector Freemantle to have overlooked such an obvious clue.

"Yes," he said, "although I wouldn't have called it obvious. The plug looked just like the wood around it. Even if you noticed it, you might not guess it had been put there as a spyhole. Pine boards are full of holes and knots." With a smile, he added, "But I have no doubt Ned will gnash his teeth just the same. I shall give you full credit for the discovery."

"Please don't," I said. "I'd rather you didn't mention my name at all." Unlike my collaboration with opera, this wasn't something I cared to be publicly linked with. It was bad enough that I was probably going to lose one of my clients over it. I didn't want to lose all of them.

He agreed reluctantly, Dear Reader. Idealist that he is, it went against the grain for him to take credit that was owing to someone else. "I shall feel it belongs to you in any case," he said. "I am in your debt for that, Seraphina, and for giving me the Toth lead as well."

He smiled as he spoke and pressed my hand, yet it was easy to see that his thoughts were now on Mrs. Henley rather than me. I was sure he was itching to question her about the spyhole. "I am glad if I could help," I told him. "But if you'll excuse me now, I must be getting back to the Temple. No, you needn't see me home, Tom. I'll be safe enough with Sam."

***

As the two of us had come together in my brougham, it was necessary to explain to Sam, my coachman, that the Inspector was staying behind to follow up a lead. Sam accepted this statement without question, as he generally does (and as I only wish Susan and Jenny would do).

When we reached home, the two of them were immensely interested to hear of my discoveries in Miss Bird's room. Susan, indeed, was so interested that she let go of the last of her resentment, and we had a lively discussion in our old style.

"My God," she said. "So you think Mr. Toth is the one who's been committing all these murders?"

"It seems at least possible," I said. "In theory, any of the Toths might have left the book and my card in that room. But he's the only one who's likely to be patronizing a place of that sort. Even if he didn't commit the murders, I can see him going there to consort with some woman he'd met on the street. He might well have had *Walden* with him, too. All the Toths treat it as though it were the Bible."

"Maybe that's why he had it with him," said Susan, grinning. "Maybe he likes to read bits of it to women by way of inspiration."

"That's practically blasphemy," I told her, "though it wouldn't be more twisted than anything else about him, to be sure."

Jenny shook her head, her expression stern. "And a spyhole in the room, too," she said. "How folks can! I'll never understand such things."

"It's a curious taste," I agreed.

"A man's taste," said Susan, disparagingly.

"Not necessarily," I said. "It would depend on the motive, of course. A man is more likely if the motive was merely prurient, but a woman might do it, too, out of curiosity. And of course either sex is possible if the motive was blackmail."

We looked at one another. "That'd be something, wouldn't it?" said Susan. "If it was a blackmailer, and he was watching the night of the murder, he got more than he bargained for. And wouldn't he have a hold on his victim then!"

"A hold on a tiger's tail," I said. "A murderer would be a lot more dangerous to blackmail than an adulterer. But of course, there's no certainty anyone was watching on that particular night. Indeed, the hole may have been put there years ago and forgotten."

Of course that wasn't what I was hoping, Dear Reader. I was hoping there had been a watcher that night whom Inspector Harper would be able to track down speedily, and whose testimony would show that some person other than Absalom Toth had killed Miss Bird. But I knew the frustrating nature of police work and wasn't surprised when he reported a few days later that Mrs. Henley disclaimed all knowledge of the spyhole.

"Do you think she's lying?" I asked.

He ran his hand through his hair. "Probably," he said. "But we haven't been able to shake her story so far. She just keeps repeating that the room next to Miss Bird's is an empty one that's never used or rented out. That in itself seems suspicious, but in fact the room *is* empty. And there's nothing to show that it was recently occupied."

"Can you do anything else?"

"We're threatening to close her business down, hoping to make her talk. So far it's not working." He looked at me humourously. "Ned's furious about it—that, and the fact that I was the one who found the spyhole. *And* found a possible suspect. Though he's behaved handsomely enough about that, on the whole. The whole force is under a lot of pressure to find out who's been committing these murders. I think we'd all be glad to have the business stopped, even if it doesn't bring us any credit personally."

"Does it look as though Mr. Toth were responsible?" I asked. I almost dreaded to voice the question, Dear Reader, yet obviously it was better I should be prepared for any repercussions.

He took his time answering. "It's hard to say," he said. "He's been questioned several times, but I can't say we've established any conclusion one way or another. He admits that the book we found was his. He admits he knew Miss Bird; that they had a physical relationship; and that he had been in the habit of coming to that room with her for the past six months or so. But he claims he wasn't there with her the night of the murder. In fact, he claims not to have known there *was* a murder, until we told him about it. He says he knew the victim only as Matty and never thought to connect her with the Matilda Bird who was killed."

"I suppose that's possible," I said.

He shook his head doubtfully. "I find it hard to believe anyone could be so oblivious. Considering the public furor these crimes have aroused, I'd expect he must have put two and two together. But then, I'm involved in the case myself, so I might be more sensitive on the subject than an outsider."

"Yes," I said. "And as outsiders go, you couldn't get much further outside than the Toths. They aren't English; they've got a set of beliefs that isolate them from the rest of humanity; and they're rich enough to keep all unpleasantness at arm's length."

"So I gathered," said the Inspector. "And in fact Mr. Toth seemed much shaken to learn that his—er—paramour had been killed. Though I'm obliged to say his concern seemed to centre less on her being murdered than the idea of his mother finding out he had been carrying on an illicit relationship with her."

That seemed perfectly in keeping with what I knew of Absalom Toth. "Does she know yet?" I asked. "His mother?"

The Inspector shook his head. "We don't go out of our way to make trouble for people," he said. "Unless and until he's charged with a crime, we'll do our best to keep his connection with the victim quiet. And I don't see any immediate likelihood of his being charged. Of course we're investigating his story and trying to establish that he was there with Miss Bird on the night of her murder. And we're looking also to see if we can connect him with any of the other murders."

"At least there shouldn't be any more murders, if he's the one who's been committing them," I said. "After being questioned by the police, he would know he was under suspicion and behave accordingly."

The Inspector smiled. "Yes," he said, "though Ned would argue otherwise. He's still clinging to his religious madman theory. He thinks that if Mr. Toth is the murderer, he won't be able to help killing again."

"If that's so, I wonder he doesn't want to put him under lock and key right now," I said. "That would be the safe thing to do, if he's likely to kill again."

"But we haven't the evidence to convict him, as matters now stand," explained the Inspector. "Ned thinks that if we give him enough rope now, he'll eventually hang himself."

I said acidly that from what I had seen of Inspector Freemantle, he would think nothing of sacrificing a couple more women's lives to prove his theory. "Oh, we're taking precautions," Inspector Harper assured me. "The dark of the moon is just a few days away, and practically the whole force will be on duty that night. We'll have men posted at likely locations, besides making extra patrols."

"Likely locations being places with religious associations?"

The Inspector laughed ruefully. "Yes, Ned's having his way about that, at least. But other places will be watched, too. And with there being so much publicity about these crimes, we'll have the public watching out as well—not to mention the women who are most at risk. They've got the biggest stake of all in the business, when you think of it."

"Yes, I expect so," I agreed. "You'd think they'd be on their guard. But I suppose there's always going to be someone desperate enough to take the risk."

"I'm afraid so," he said soberly.

I envisioned the streets, lit only by gaslight, with a dark figure prowling about in search of his next victim—while the police desperately sought to find him first. There was something exciting in the idea, Dear Reader. I half wished I were part of the search myself. "Is there anything I could do to help?" I asked.

He thanked me, but said he thought the police had the situation well in hand this time. "Though I suppose you might consult the Spirits," he added, eying me quizzically. "Just to see if we're overlooking some obvious clue."

By Spirits, he meant my private sources of information. "That's an idea," I said. "I might do that. I'll let you know if I receive any Spiritual Communications that might bear on your investigation."

He thanked me again, smiling. "Just send a note around if you do. I'm afraid I won't be able to visit you for the next few days. The Chief wants most of us on night patrol from here on out, just in case the fellow anticipates the dark of the moon by a day or two."

I told him I wished him all possible luck. "I hope you personally succeed in capturing the murderer, Tom."

"I'm afraid that'd be too much luck to hope for," he said, laughing. "But I suppose it's barely possible." With a roguish look, he added, "Perhaps you wouldn't have any objection to kissing me—just for luck, you know?"

I said that as it was a matter of ensuring public safety, I thought I could accede to his request. He seemed gratified. At any rate, when he took leave of me a short time later, he assured me he felt certain now of not only collaring the murderer singlehandedly but of being made Chief Inspector in very short order.

Chapter 8

The next day, I acted on the Inspector's suggestion and sought advice from the Spirits. That is to say, I put on my best hat, called for Sam and the carriage, and went to visit Felicity, who is as close to an oracle as one can find in these degenerate days.

Just as I have my Temple of Spiritualism, so Felicity has her own place of business: The Calico Cat. To the uninitiated, the Cat appears a simple tea-shop, dark and low-beamed and slightly shabby in its appointments. One can get a very good tea there, however. And it is also the place to go if you want to consult Felicity, perhaps the most knowing woman in London as well as the chief of the agents who bring me information.

I found Felicity in her favourite place by the fire, from which she can scrutinize all visitors to the shop (and take drastic measures against any who might be unwelcome). I had to look twice before I recognized her. Felicity's appearance changes drastically from day to day, depending on what business she has in hand. Today she was grand as a duchess in a silk dress quite as good as my own, a set of furs only slightly touched by the moth, and a high-crowned hat bristling with plumes.

"My dear Seraphina," she said, waving me toward the empty chair opposite her. "Do sit down and have a cup of tea with me." In keeping with her costume, her accents were refined enough for a duchess—indeed, a good deal more refined than some duchesses I could name.

"My dear Felicity," I returned, taking the chair. "I should be delighted."

I waited while she summoned the attendant to bring fresh scones and another cup. Once the girl departed with the order, she leaned forward to address me in her normal businesslike accents.

"Got what you were wanting, dear," she said. "From that place in Berkeley Square. The matter's just as you thought."

"Excellently done," I approved. The matter she spoke of concerned another of my clients, whose home she had managed to enter under one of her many guises and from whose servants she had obtained some confidential information. She has a genius for this kind of work, Dear Reader. It would not be too much to call her a complete genius, like Mr. Witters, though of a rather different sort. Whether it be as a seller of cheapjack merchandise, a servant in search of work, a beggar seeking alms, or (as in the present instance) a seeming duchess, Felicity can inveigle her way into the most unlikely places.

We talked a little more about other matters while drinking numerous cups of tea. I was just considering how best to introduce the subject of the murders when Felicity introduced it herself.

"I wish that inspector of yours would get busy and find this bastard who's cutting women's throats," she said. "Putting a regular crimp in my business, he is."

I remarked sympathetically that people naturally wouldn't like to venture out when there was a murderer about. Felicity said this was true, although not her primary concern. "All these police," she explained, "and not just uniformed coppers, but plainclothesmen, too. It isn't playing fair to *my* way of thinking. And all of them running about and poking their noses in places where they've no cause to be. It's very vexing to folk who just want to be let alone to go about their business."

I could see that it *would* be vexing, considering the kinds of business Felicity is involved in. Insinuating her way into people's houses to get information is the very least of it. "You've no idea who the murderer might be?" I asked. "No one has said anything to you that might be a clue to his identity?'

She shook her head grimly. "If I did know," she said, "he'd have been stopped long before this, *and* with no need for the police. Nor the hangman neither."

I had no trouble believing it, Dear Reader. Felicity's natural appearance is sweet and motherly, but only a fool would dismiss her on those grounds. Maternal instincts can be uncommonly fierce. Think of a mother bear defending her cubs, or a lioness her young. I myself would sooner face a lioness in her den than cross Felicity on her own particular turf.

"You don't know anything yourself?" she asked me in turn. "Your inspector hasn't let drop anything when he's been with you?"

I did not answer at once, which was answer enough for someone as sharp as she is. "What did he say?" she demanded. "Do the police know who it is?" In her excitement she half rose from her chair, causing one or two people in the shop to look at her before averting their eyes with an air of belated prudence.

"They don't *know*," I said. "But they do have a suspect. I myself brought him to their attention. He happens to be a client of mine."

Felicity was already opening her mouth to ask the inevitable question. I hurriedly forestalled her. "It's not at all certain he's the murderer," I said. "All we know for certain is that he was one of Matilda Bird's—ahem—customers. And that he had been in the room where she was murdered on other occasions."

Felicity was of the opinion that this was evidence enough. I had to argue long and hard and make her swear not to execute immediate vengeance before I was willing to reveal Mr. Toth's name. "The police are investigating his connection with the other crimes as well as trying to prove he was in Miss Bird's room on the night she was killed," I assured her. "I don't think there's any chance of his going free if he's really the murderer."

As a matter of interest, I told her also about the spyhole in Miss Bird's room. It was easy to see that Felicity *was* interested. She made me tell her twice about my experiences that afternoon. "You say a woman named Henley let you in," she said. "That'd be Peg Henley, I've no doubt. I haven't had any dealings with her myself, but I do recollect hearing someone of that name was running an accommodation house in Bermondsey."

The Toths she was not acquainted with at all, Dear Reader. This was not surprising. Because they were Americans and their

Spirit was a literary one, I had been forced to use other agents and unorthodox lines of investigation rather than employing her. She questioned me minutely about them and their affairs, to the point that I began to worry whether I might not soon have Mr. Toth's blood on my hands. There is, they say, honour among thieves, but I did not know how far her vow would restrain her if she believed him guilty of the murders.

"At least let the police conduct their own investigation first," I urged. "Time enough to pursue other measures if they fail."

She agreed, but in a cagey manner that did not altogether reassure me. "It won't hurt for me to ask a few questions, anyway," she said.

I reminded her that the police were already asking questions, and that she might draw their attention if she was going about doing the same thing. With an air of scorn, she responded, "The people *I* know won't talk to the police. Never you fear, dear: I'll take precautions. The police'll never know I lifted a finger in the matter, unless I want them to."

With this I had to be satisfied, Dear Reader. I went back to the Temple with the uneasy feeling that I might have set forces into motion that I could not stop.

***

The next few days were uneventful as to crime, though interesting in other ways. I finished the lyrics for *Night and Day,* spent an afternoon with Mr. Witters arguing out details of dialogue, and paid a visit to the opera house, where casting for the piece had begun.

Signora Mazzara was in her element, abusing all and sundry when they fell afoul of her temper. To do her justice, however, she was equally vociferous in praise when something pleased her. She was pleased with the selection of Mr. Benjamin Cardle (tenor) for Lucien, her love interest. She was also pleased to approve the selection of Signor Nino Adriano (baritone) for the treacherous Apollo. But the casting of Susan/Egeria tried her temper. You may remember, Dear Reader, that she had stipulated this rôle be played by an older woman. Unfortunately, the part fell instead to Miss Edith Dart, a fair-haired Englishwoman some years younger than the signora herself.

"She is all wrong for the rôle," said the signora dismissively. "For one thing, she is English, and it is well known that the English are cold and without passion. They have no aptitude for grand opera."

Mr. Hinney unwisely pointed out that Mr. Cardle was also English and got called a son of a dog and a *maledetto bastardo* for his pains. "Mr. Cardle, though English, is *simpatico*. This Englishwoman is not."

In response, Mr. Hinney undertook a defence of Miss Dart's sympathetic qualities—a defence rather undermined by Miss Dart herself, who was looking down her nose at the signora with unmistakable disdain. "You'll see, Paola. Her voice has just the quality to bring out the best qualities of your own."

The signora made a noise dismissive of Miss Dart's vocal qualities. "How can this woman play my trusted friend and advisor?" she demanded. "She is too insignificant—too childish—altogether too lacking in presence."

The words "too young," were not mentioned, but the inference was plain. Mr. Hinney, with a glance at his assistant, said costuming and makeup could do a lot to give Miss Dart the necessary air of age and wisdom. "I'll have the costume people confer with you, Paola. One way or another, we'll make certain she looks the part."

The signora, after due deliberation, agreed to this compromise. From her satisfied smile, I felt pretty sure that she was visualizing Miss Dart swathed in veils from head to toe.

The score was in its very early stages, but Mr. Witters had gotten the signora's second act aria sketched out, and she ran through it a few times to piano accompaniment. It was gratifying to hear my words set to music, even if a lot of them were, technically, Henry David Thoreau's words. She managed the high A every time. I saw Mr. Hinney and Mr. Witters exchange looks expressive of relief and satisfaction.

I was so diverted by the whole business that it wasn't until I was driving home that I remembered tonight was the dark of the moon.

Chapter 9

When I reached the Temple, I had just time for a cup of tea and a biscuit before my sitting.

I glanced through the evening newspapers as I drank my tea. Judging by the headlines, I was the only one in London to have forgotten, even for a moment, that it was the dark of the moon. Without exception, the front pages were given over to discussion of the New Moon Murderer (as the press had dubbed him) and speculation as to whether he would claim another victim that night.

For my part, I doubted it. If Felicity found extra police on the streets hampering to *her* business, it stood to reason that the murderer must be suffering under the same restraint. Not only that, but he was likely to find victims scarce now that word had spread about his activities. Unless he really was a madman, he would probably decide to skip a few months until the furor had died down, or at least choose a different phase of the moon for his next crime.

All that evening, as I sat spelling out answers on the Spiritograph, I kept thinking of Inspector Harper. I envisioned him lurking in the shadows of some squalid court, or loitering beneath a streetlamp in the dress of a tramp or day-labourer. I hoped he might have luck enough to be hot on the trail of the murderer.

It was fortunate that I was sitting that evening for Lady Haverhill, one of my regular and least demanding clients. On a weekly basis, I summon up the Spirit of her late husband so she can bully and berate him in Death even as she did in Life. About ninety-nine percent of his responses are simply the equivalent of "Yes, dear" and require no thought at all on my part. Given my distracted state of mind, it was just as well.

Certainly it was just as well I was not sitting for the Toths.

I was glad, nonetheless, when the sitting was over. After bidding Lady Haverhill good-night, I went upstairs to change into more comfortable attire for my usual supper conference with Susan and Jenny.

My mind was still full of Inspector Harper and the murders as I threw open my bedroom door. That in no way prepared me for what happened next, however. As I stepped into the dark room, an arm went around my neck and I felt the prick of a blade against my chin. "Don't move," whispered a voice. "Don't move, or I'll cut your throat."

In moments of stress or excitement, Dear Reader, time seems to behave in a curious fashion. And in *that* moment, a whole lifetime's worth of thoughts flashed through my mind. I reflected that I was about to die, undoubtedly a victim of the same murderer who had been terrorizing London these last few months. It was too much of a coincidence that I should be killed by an unrelated assailant wielding a knife. My mind coolly rejected the hypothesis after only the briefest consideration.

I reflected also that in so dying, I would undoubtedly be ranked as a prostitute like the other victims. This was patently unjust, and even in the extremity of that moment I resented it.

I reflected also that I was about to die without Inspector Harper ever making love to me. This was yet another cause for resentment. Perhaps he would regret his foolish reticence when he found my lifeless body lying in a pool of blood on my bedroom floor. Undoubtedly, he would be grieved by my death.

The idea of his grief made me feel more generous, Dear Reader. I found myself hoping he might at least have the compensation of bringing my killer to justice—and perhaps be promoted to Chief Inspector as a result. I further reflected that I might even help him, if I dared. If I were to scream now, as loudly as I could, it might cause the killer to cut my throat immediately, but it also would increase the likelihood of some member of my household catching him before he could get away.

At about this point in my reflections, it dawned on me to wonder why I hadn't been killed already. I could hear my assailant's breathing, quick and shallow, and feel the trembling of the hand that held the knife against my throat. That seemed odd. Surely a man who had killed five women would not hesitate to kill a sixth. Could he possibly be having doubts?

At that moment, he spoke in a grating whisper: "You," he said, "you should have stayed out of what doesn't concern you."

For answer, I opened my mouth and screamed.

I cannot reach the pitch of A over high C, Dear Reader, but I gave it all I was worth. I fully expected to feel the knife slash into my throat every second. But instead it was whipped away with a speed that was shocking in a different way. An instant later, I heard feet pounding down the stairs. I ran to the landing and looked down, just in time to catch a glimpse of a dark-clad figure making for the side door.

"Damn," I said, feeling my throat to make sure it was still intact. "Damn, damn, damn."

I had hardly done speaking when Susan appeared at the top of the stairs. She was followed an instant later by Jenny and Sam. "What on earth is the matter?" she demanded.

"We heard you screaming, ma'am," explained Jenny. Sam, for his part, said nothing, but stood with his eyes fixed on me, waiting for my answer.

I told them what had happened. Three pairs of eyes opened wide, and three mouths gaped in astonishment.

"The murderer, here?" exclaimed Jenny.

"But how did he get in?" demanded Susan.

Sam said nothing, but headed down the stairs with a purposeful tread. "Sam, come back," I called. "He's got too much of a start. I doubt we'll catch him now. Besides, we have more important things to do."

"Fetch the police, you mean?" asked Jenny.

"We'll have to do that eventually," I agreed. "But first we must put the place in order for them."

Susan caught on immediately. "We'll need to swap the dummy Spiritograph for the other," she said.

"*And* disable the real one. Sam, help me, please." Together we went down to the Spirit Parlour and unbolted the box from the table base, exposing the battery compartment beneath. Sam carefully lifted out the batteries in their glass jars and looked to me for instruction. "You'll need to hide them somewhere the police won't be likely to find them," I said. "And also the box with the wheel and bell."

Susan suggested the kitchen might be a good place. "Jenny and I between us have been there all afternoon and evening, so we can swear the murderer didn't get in that way. Likely the police won't search it too closely in that case."

I approved this idea. "Put the batteries at the back of the pantry and stack some tinned and bottled goods in front. With luck, they'll be taken as jars of preserves or pickles." Although I was technically a victim of this crime, I didn't want to leave anything lying around that might cause the police to question my own activities. I trusted they wouldn't feel it necessary to search my premises too closely, but there was no sense taking chances. If nothing else, it would be embarrassing for Inspector Harper, now publicly my friend, to have me exposed as a fraud.

Fortunately, I had made provision for this situation long ago by having a dummy Spiritograph table made, identical in appearance to the real one but lacking any electrical mechanism. We moved this dummy table into the Spirit Parlour from my study, put the real table (now denuded of its apparatus) in its place, threw a cloth over it, and covered its surface with books and papers. I also disconnected the wiring for the bell that rang in the stables. It would be a vexing amount of labour to put everything right again afterwards, but I felt I would rather not leave anything about to suggest other electric equipment on the premises.

I will say now, Dear Reader, that my concern was needless. When the police arrived, they focused their attention almost exclusively on my bedroom, where the killer had hidden himself, and on my side door, where he had presumably gotten in. They didn't search the kitchen at all, nor did they make more than a cursory search of the stable, where (it later developed) Sam had hidden the working parts of the Spiritograph, wrapped in oilcloth and concealed beneath a pile of manure. Possibly it was an association of ideas, although I tend to think that kind of satirical comment is beyond Sam.

Even without any inquiry into my business, it was a long and trying night. I never even had a chance to change out of my evening dress. The police did not leave my bedroom until dawn was breaking over the city. The fact that Inspector Harper was among the investigating officers was of surprisingly little consolation. In all the possible scenarios in which I might have envisioned him spending the night in my bedroom, that one had never occurred to me.

The added presence of Inspector Freemantle was in no way an improvement to the scenario, as far as I was concerned.

"You're sure you weren't mistaken, ma'am?" he asked me, for at least the third or fourth time. "You're sure the fellow had a knife?"

"Very sure," I said, my hand going involuntarily to my throat. "I felt it, and I could see it, too—the hilt of it, at least. And his hand holding it."

Inspector Freemantle wrote something in his notebook, but with an air of still not believing me. "I don't see how it could be related to *our* business," he told Inspector Harper. "Even if she's right, and the fellow did hold a knife to her throat, it doesn't fit."

"She's certainly not the typical victim," said Inspector Harper (I was impressed with his gentlemanly concern for my reputation, Dear Reader, even at a moment like this). "But apart from that, it fits well enough."

"But there's no religious association," argued Inspector Freemantle. "That's been a unifying point in all the other murders."

"So you say," said Inspector Harper with a weary air. "And it may be you are right, Ned. But as I was telling Madame Fox earlier, that would not necessarily exclude an attack on her. For this place is called the Temple of Spiritualism, after all."

Inspector Freemantle seemed hardly to hear him. "I still think she must be mistaken," he insisted. "I had a strong notion that tonight's attack might take place around Spitalsfields—in the vicinity of the old priory, perhaps, or another place with a religious association."

"This place is called a *temple*, Ned," said Inspector Harper patiently. "That's a religious place, too."

"Oh," said Inspector Freemantle. He looked at me again, as if for the first time. "By jingo, so it is." In a voice of growing enthusiasm, he added, "Well, then, that's clear enough." As well as enthusiasm, there was a note of speculation in his voice, which I had no difficulty interpreting. Since the other victims had been prostitutes, it followed that I must be one also.

I could see, too, that the appearance of my bedroom did nothing to allay his suspicions. I have done well for myself these past few years, Dear Reader, and have been able to indulge my fancy as to bedroom décor. There was nothing so blatant as a mirror on the ceiling, but even so it did not look exactly like the chaste bedchamber of a maiden lady. I saw Inspector Freemantle's eyes flickering from my double bed with its draperies of plum-coloured chiffon, to my dressing table laden with bottles of scent and cosmetics, to the triple looking-glass and wardrobe bursting with elaborate costumes in silk and satin, and could guess exactly the conclusions he was drawing.

Inspector Harper obviously guessed them, too, for he began at once to stress how my attack had differed from the others. "The whole business seems more in the nature of a threat than a failed attack," he told his colleague. Turning to me, he asked, "Didn't you say the man spoke as though he were there in retaliation for some action of yours?"

"Yes," I said. "He said I shouldn't have interfered in business that didn't concern me."

The two detectives exchanged glances. "It must be the Toth connection," said Inspector Harper. "It's the only way she touches this affair."

"Seems to be," said Inspector Freemantle, still eyeing me speculatively. "I don't know, though. How would he know it was her that blew the gaff on him? We took care not to reveal that when we were questioning him."

"He guessed it, of course," said Inspector Harper. "Which means it was he who attacked her tonight."

Inspector Freemantle looked doubtful. "No-o-o-o," he said, drawing out the word to several syllables. "I hardly see how it could have been him. For it happens I was shadowing him tonight—I and one of my men."

"You were?" said Inspector Harper, looking startled. "You didn't mention that before, Ned. So it couldn't have been Toth who was here tonight?"

Inspector Freemantle did not reply for a moment. He threw me another look, not so much speculative this time as ill-at-ease. "It's a complicated business," he said finally. "Wait until we get back to the Yard, Tom, and we can discuss it further."

It was obvious that he did not want to speak in front of me. "If you are done questioning me," I said, with elaborate courtesy, "perhaps I might go down to the kitchen and see how my servants are faring?"

"Certainly," said Inspector Harper, with another glance at his colleague. "I think we're done questioning you for tonight. Go on downstairs, and I'll come down and let you know when we've finished up here."

***

I found Susan, Jenny, and Sam seated at the kitchen table along with a uniformed constable whom I recognized as P.C. Shaw, an old friend of ours. [13] I hailed him familiarly as I sat down at the table with the four of them. "Is there any chance of something to eat?" I asked Susan. "I'm completely and utterly famished."

"Lord, yes," she said. "You've had no supper, and no more have the rest of us. I forgot all about it in the excitement. It's only cold meat and bread and cheese, though," she added, rising to her feet, "so no harm done."

She fetched the cold meat and bread and cheese, and we all tucked in. Even P.C. Shaw had a morsel of bread and cheese

---

[13] See *Ghost in the Machine*

for old times' sake. "Do the police have any idea how the murderer got in?" I asked, looking from him to the others.

Susan glanced at Jenny, who hung her head. "I'm sorry, ma'am," she said. "I reckon it was my fault. We had the coal man come today, and I left the side door open while I went around to make sure the bin got locked up after. I never dreamed anybody could have got inside, just in that little time."

"Of course not," I said, reaching over to pat her hand. "Whoever *could* have expected such a thing? He must have been hanging about, waiting for an opportunity to slip in. And if he hadn't got in then, he would doubtless have taken some other way."

"They're going to question Lady Haverhill's servants, too," put in Susan. "There's always a chance he slipped in while your sitting was going on. The coachman went out a couple of times to see to the horses, so we know the side door was open then."

I nodded glumly. Here was another of my clients to be harassed by the police. Still, I reckoned Lady Haverhill would take it in stride if anybody could. "If he came in while you were busy with the coal man, he must have been hiding in my bedroom all afternoon and evening," I observed aloud. "And what a nasty thought *that* is!"

"Do you think it was Mr. Toth?" asked Jenny in a low voice.

Inspector Harper had asked me the same question, Dear Reader. I had had trouble answering it then, too. "I can't be sure," I said. "I only got a glimpse of him when he was running away. He had some kind of a hood or mask over his head. He was about the right height and build, I think, but I can't say much more than that."

"It's a wonder you weren't killed," observed Susan. "It's as I've said before: you've the Devil's own luck."

"I don't think it was luck," I said, reaching up to touch my throat once more. "There was nothing to stop him killing me in the first moment if he had wanted to. Instead he just stood there, with the knife to my throat. Inspector Harper thinks he might have meant it as a warning."

We all considered this. "Seems likely," said Susan, with a nod. "Well, I don't suppose you'll be sitting for the Toths any more after this. The police are bound to arrest Mr. Toth now, I should think."

"That depends," I said, with a guarded look at P.C. Shaw. "Inspector Freemantle spoke as though Mr. Toth couldn't have been responsible for this business tonight. Perhaps we will learn more once the police have had time to sift the matter to the bottom."

Chapter 10

As might be expected, the police didn't get the matter sifted to the bottom that night. In fact, their preliminary investigation seemed to have produced more questions than answers. This I learned from Inspector Harper when he came to take leave of me around dawn.

"Is it true that Absalom Toth couldn't have been the one who attacked me?" I asked. "Since Inspector Freemantle and his men were following him at the time?"

He shook his head, looking worried. "It seems unlikely, but there's still an outside chance. It appears Toth managed to give our men the slip last night. Whether by accident or design, he met up with another man who was about the same height and build and dressed much the same. Ned was following along behind with P.C. Cobden, so they kept on following, keeping both men in sight. But then they separated, and it wasn't clear which was which. So Ned followed one of them, and Cobden, who's a young man, new to that kind of work, took the other."

It didn't take much psychic ability to guess what had happened next, Dear Reader. "And Cobden lost him," I said flatly.

The Inspector nodded. "Ned found out pretty quickly *his* man wasn't Toth. So he abandoned the chase and went back to find Cobden. But when he caught up with him, he found Cobden had lost Toth's trail and was wandering around in circles. The two of them couldn't find any further trace of him. And while they were casting about, still trying to find him, they received word of *your* being attacked. The rest you know."

"So he could have come here after all?"

"It seems unlikely," said the Inspector again, in a voice that struck me as slightly evasive. "The times are very tight. At least, they're tight if Ned is accurate in his recollections. He seemed a little uncertain when we were talking just now." In a more reassuring voice, he added, "But we'll find Toth, if he's still in London. It isn't possible that he can escape us now."

***

In the days that followed, no word about my attack appeared in the newspapers. I supposed the police must be keeping that information private for reasons of their own. Perhaps they were hoping that a New Moon passing with no new victim would reassure the public that their efforts were paying off.

If so, their hopes weren't answered. The newspapers, while expressing relief that there had been no new murder, were nonetheless highly critical that no progress had been made toward finding the perpetrator of the other murders. Indeed, from their standpoint, the one situation was as unsatisfactory as the other. A new murder would have at least given them something exciting to write about.

And then it turned out they *did* have something exciting to write about. For a few days after that night—the night that was such an eventful one for me and my household—the body of a woman was discovered in a churchyard in Poplar. The medical evidence showed that her throat had been slashed some days earlier. Given this fact, and the fact that the woman was known to have earned her living as a prostitute, it seemed only too likely that she had died during the dark of the moon like her sisters.

I got the news sooner than the newspapers, thanks to Inspector Harper. He called around teatime to tell me what had happened. "Could Absalom Toth have done it?" I asked.

He ran his fingers through his hair, always a sign of mental perturbation with him. "I'm damned if I know," he said. "It's turning out to be a devil of a case. I'm not sure if I'm on my head or heels."

I begged him to be more explicit. "The last I heard, you were trying to determine if Mr. Toth had time to come here, after giving Inspector Freemantle the slip."

"Yes," he said. "And that's where the difficulty lies. It happens that the churchyard where we found the latest victim wasn't far from the place where Ned lost track of Toth that night."

"Ah," I said, "*that* seems clear enough." The next moment, however, a doubt occurred to me. "But if he was murdering a woman in Poplar—"

"—then he couldn't have been holding a knife to your throat here," finished the Inspector. "I don't see any way the times can be made to fit. Especially since Toth has an alibi for that night."

"An alibi?"

"*Two* alibis, in fact. Although the one cancels the other out, to some extent." He laughed mirthlessly.

Again I begged him to be more explicit. "Does he have an alibi or not?"

"Well," said the Inspector, looking wryly amused, "*you* be the judge. In the first place, his sister, Miss Ernestine Toth, swears he never left the house at all that night. She claims they spent the whole evening together, and then, according to her, they both went to bed early. And she is certain he did not go out at any time during the night."

I stared at him, trying to make sense of this. "She must be lying," I said. "At least, she must be if Inspector Freemantle saw him near the churchyard that night."

"Yes," said Inspector Harper. "But you'll recall there was some confusion about that. Ned Freemantle saw him *and another man who closely resembled him.* Can't you see how that complicates matters? For if Ned couldn't say for certain which one was Toth, he couldn't swear *either* of them was Toth. The one point compromises the other. If it ever came to trial, Toth's defence would tear it to shreds."

"Oh," I said blankly.

"And then we come to the matter of the second alibi," continued Inspector Harper. "Mr. Toth himself claims he *was* out that night, and in the neighbourhood of Poplar, too. But instead of murdering a prostitute in a churchyard, he claims to have been consorting with a live one in a bawdy house. A Miss Elsie Rattle, in fact. And Miss Rattle, along with two or three others that were there that night, is willing to swear that he arrived well before midnight—just about the time Ned and P.C. Cobden lost sight of him. *And* that he remained there till morning. Which means he couldn't have been the one who attacked *you.*"

"Oh," I said again. "I can't make sense of it at all!"

"And of course, this poor girl who was just killed—Lizzy Gowd—we can't positively prove she was killed that night. The presumption is strong, but her body had been lying about long enough that the doctors aren't willing to pin it down to a specific day or time. So—Toth might have murdered her. He might even have murdered her that night. But if he did, he must have done it in a matter of minutes without getting a drop of blood on his clothing. He must then have disposed of the knife somehow and gone on to his rendezvous with Miss Rattle without showing any sign of physical or mental perturbation."

I thought hard, trying again to make sense of all this. "Perhaps Miss Rattle is lying," I said. "She and the others."

"Perhaps," said the Inspector. "But I don't think they are. Their stories sounded quite natural and circumstantial. I didn't get the sense they'd been rehearsed beforehand. And certainly they seemed much more genuine than Miss Toth's!"

"Yes," I said. "Obviously *she's* lying. And it's equally obvious why, of course. She must know about her brother's nocturnal activities and be trying to protect him. From her mother, probably, as much as the police."

"Likely enough," agreed the Inspector.

"So Mr. Toth *might* have killed Miss Gowd. But probably not on the dark of the moon. *Or* she might have been killed by someone else, either then or at another time."

"That's it in a nutshell," agreed the Inspector.

I thought the situation over some more. "I still think Mr. Toth must have done it," I said. "It seems too much of a coincidence that he was in the neighbourhood that night and a corpse found not long after. We already know that whoever's been committing these crimes is ruthless and cold-blooded. Very likely he *could* kill one woman and go on to a tryst with another immediately afterward."

"Possibly," said the Inspector. "But then who attacked you?"

I was still loath to accept the idea that my attack could be an unrelated matter. "That could be Mr. Toth, too, if Miss Rattle is lying," I said.

"*And* her employer, and her employer's maidservant?" returned the Inspector.

"Perhaps he set the clock back—convinced them all he came in earlier than he did?"

The Inspector shook his head. "It still doesn't fit," he said. "Not for *your* attack. Remember Ned and Cobden were trailing Toth around the time that took place. He couldn't have got from there to here in the time."

"It doesn't make sense," I said with vexation. Then suddenly another thought occurred to me. "The other man!" I said. "The one Inspector Freemantle was trailing."

He smiled. "Yes," he said. "I wondered when you'd think of that."

"He must have resembled Absalom Toth closely, or he wouldn't have deceived Inspector Freemantle," I said, reasoning aloud. "Perhaps it was really he who spent the night with Miss Rattle!"

The Inspector shook his head. "I don't think that can be the case. Toth's an unusual-looking fellow, as you well know. It would be hard to mistake him for anyone else face-to-face. And it seems Miss Rattle has been—er—on intimate terms with him for some months."

I remarked acidly that Mr. Toth certainly spread his favours around. "Very well, it was he with Miss Rattle. That means it must have been the other man who came here—*before* he met Toth on the street. Tom, that would fit!"

"Yes," he agreed. "But who was he, and what was his relationship with Toth?"

"Perhaps they both have been in the business all along," I suggested. "Maybe the murders have been committed by *two* men, not one."

Inspector Harper received this suggestion without enthusiasm. "It's possible," he said. "At least it would explain why all our trails go in circles or wind up in dead ends."

"Or perhaps Mr. Toth simply hired the other man to threaten me and provide an alibi for himself at the same time."

"He might have hired him to threaten you," said Inspector Harper. "But he didn't hire him for an alibi. Because Toth claims he didn't meet any other man that night. He claims he was completely alone during his walk to Miss Rattle's."

I stared at him. "But why would he say that? Oh, I see—if he and the other man really are in collusion, then he *would* deny having met him. But didn't Inspector Freemantle tell him he'd been seen with the other man?"

"Oh, yes," said Inspector Harper. "Ned was hammering away at him for most of the night, trying to get him to admit it."

"And did he?"

"No," said Inspector Harper. "He denied it with every appearance of sincerity. Said, when pressed, that he could remember seeing one or two men on the streets that night, but denied exchanging a word with any of them. Even described one of the men he had seen—whose appearance happened to tally precisely with P.C. Cobden's, I might add!"

I suggested that Police Constable Cobden might be better employed in some other capacity than shadowing suspects, and Inspector Harper agreed. "Not his métier, poor fellow. Toth certainly saw him—saw him well enough to describe him in some detail. He also mentioned one or two women he'd seen during his walk whom he could describe in detail, too. One he even claims to have spoken to."

"I expect I can guess the subject of the conversation," I said.

"We're trying to locate them," continued the Inspector. "They might be valuable witnesses if they saw the man who was with Toth and could describe him. But it's all very uncertain. Nothing like enough to build a case on."

I could see that this must be true. "I'm sorry, Tom," I said. "Such a lot of work, and nothing to show for it."

"Well, we're used to that," he returned. "But in a case like this, it does rather gall one." Glancing at his watch, he said he must be getting back to the Yard.

I told him to wait and let Susan make up a packet of sandwiches to take with him. "For later," I explained. "I expect Mrs. McIntyre has been stinting you again. You're looking a bit fine-drawn."

He admitted he had been obliged to forgo breakfast again that morning, but insisted it was no matter. "If I'm looking fine-drawn, it's because of this business," he said. "I don't like to think that someone can come here and hold a knife to your throat and then escape without any consequences. It touches me on the quick, professionally as well as personally."

I said I was none the worse for the experience, as he could see for himself. After that, the conversation took a more personal turn. The idea that I had been in mortal danger appeared to have stimulated him strongly. Or perhaps that night spent in my bedroom had had some positive effect after all.

"If you were to marry me," he murmured in an insinuating voice as we took leave of each other at the door, "you would automatically acquire police protection—especially during those night-time hours when danger is most threatening."

"If I were to marry you," I responded, "it would be solely for the pleasure of taking you away from Mrs. McIntyre."

This sally proved tactically unsound, Dear Reader. He instantly signified his willingness to marry me on those or any other terms I might propose. Indeed, having given what amounted to a conditional acceptance, I had a hard time fighting my way back to neutral ground.

Perhaps it was just as well that Susan appeared when she did with the sandwiches. What with one thing and another, he was being dangerously persuasive.

Chapter 11

As the Toth business appeared to be at a stalemate, I tried to turn my attention to other matters. But I did not find it easy to forget that knife pressed to my throat. I found myself remembering it at odd moments—whenever I entered a dark room, for instance, or if I heard a noise when I was lying in bed late at night.

Although I continued to reject Inspector Harper's offer of matrimony combined with police protection, I did take precautions. My assailant might have meant his visit only as a warning, but I couldn't be sure of that. My household was under strict orders to keep all doors locked and windows fastened, and Sam and Jenny moved temporarily from their flat above the stable and started sleeping in the kitchen chamber where they would be nearer to hand in case of trouble.

I took more personal measures, too. I had a police whistle Inspector Harper had given me long ago which I wore like a talisman around my neck. I had another talisman, too, from a more adventurous period in my life: my Colt revolver. It was a thoroughly bothersome thing to carry, Dear Reader, being far too heavy and bulky to keep in a pocket or handbag. I had fashioned a kind of suspender-holster that hung from my waist, which I could reach through a strategically-located slit in my skirt. Cumbersome as it was to have the thing slapping against my thigh all day, its presence was still a comfort. As a weapon it would trump a knife—and it was the only weapon that would enable me to keep an assailant at more than arm's length.

Thus fortified, I went about my daily business, which was largely opera-centred just then. Rehearsals of *Night and Day* had begun, and I found great charm in seeing the child of my brain take shape onstage. The singing, dancing, and acting were all enjoyable to watch, but even more I enjoyed watching the workmen build the sets and use lights, coloured gauze, and steam to create magical effects. I watched, listened, and asked questions, storing away a few ideas that I thought I might later adapt to my Spirit Parlour.

Signora Mazzara was, of course, Queen Bee in this hive of activity. Mr. Hinney told me in confidence that she was growing quite reconciled to Edith Dart, the contralto who was playing Susan/Egeria. This hopeful pronouncement was contradicted by a nasty spat that developed between the two of them during a rehearsal of their second-act duet. Breaking off in mid-measure, the signora furiously declared that Miss Dart had no stage presence; accused her of walking through her part like a wooden puppet; and further denominated her a *meretrice* and a *maledetta bastarda*.

"I'm afraid I don't know what any of those things are," said Miss Dart with an icy smile. "You must remember that *I* am a *lady*."

Mr. Hinney hastily averted further fireworks by suggesting that they run through the piece again. Even I, a musical amateur, could hear how gloriously the two voices intertwined. For my part, I think the lower tones of the contralto voice even prettier than the higher ones of the soprano, Dear Reader—but then perhaps I might be prejudiced.

I also got to hear again the signora's second act aria, "Do You Not Dream?" Gripping the hands of Mr. Cardle (Lucien) and gazing into his eyes with passionate intensity, she sang:

"The brilliance of light
Can deceive like the night
For the eyes it may dazzle and blind;
Close your eyes, love, and see
How plain truth's shape can be
When you see with the eyes of the mind."

"*That's* going to be a winner," Mr. Hinney told me with satisfaction. "Very nice indeed."

I told Susan and Jenny about it during our conference that evening. "They have made a pretty thing of the airship for the first and final scenes," I said. "It's rigged up in the flies over the stage, and they swing it in from the wings. It looks as though it's really flying."

"And do people really ride in it?" asked Jenny.

"Just the two male principals—Lucien and Apollo. The other men are waiting in the wings, and once the ship has landed, they file in as though they had been riding in it, too. It's not big enough or sturdy enough to hold all of them. Indeed, there's some question as to whether it's sturdy enough to hold just Lucien and Apollo! They are both on the stout side, especially Mr.

Cardle, the tenor who plays Lucien." That is one of the curiosities of opera, Dear Reader. A stout, middle-aged man can play an athletic young hero, or a young lady like Miss Dart an elderly woman. The audience is expected to take it all in stride. I cannot say I disapprove; it meshes with my long-held principle that appearances are often deceptive.

Susan opined that the rehearsal sounded entertaining enough, especially the signora's histrionics. "But I wonder they put up with that sort of thing—her swearing at the other singers, I mean. What did you say she called Miss Dart?"

"A *maledetta bastarda*. I take it that's the feminine version of a *maledetto bastardo,* which is what she called Mr. Hinney once or twice. Not to mention Mr. Witters, and a couple of stagehands, and the boy who supplies the props."

"*Bastardo,*" repeated Jenny, rolling the word experimentally across her tongue. "Do you suppose that's the same as English for—"

"Yes," I said. "Almost certainly."

Susan sniffed. "Then I agree with Miss Dart," she said. "A lady oughtn't to use such language."

I agreed it wasn't ladylike language, strictly speaking. "Though of course such things sound much better in Italian than in English. Quite musical, in fact. French, as a language, has the same peculiarity. When I was living in Paris years ago—"

Susan broke in on my linguistic discourse to say that I had a note. "The Inspector brought it by earlier, during your sitting."

I tore open the note and devoured its contents. Of course any missive from the Inspector was interesting to me personally, but I had an interest as well in the progress of his case—even more than the rest of London. Every day I hoped to hear of some development that would put the New Moon Murderer behind bars, and every day I had been disappointed. I was doomed to disappointment this time, too. "Nothing," I said. "No new leads. And none of the old ones leading anywhere, either."

Susan shook her head. "And it'll be the dark of the moon again pretty soon," she said.

"And Mr. Toth is still free," I said gloomily. "They can't prove he had anything to do with Miss Gowd's death, any more than Miss Bird's. And they haven't got any further clue to the second man, either—the man whom we think might have attacked me."

"What about that spyhole you and the Inspector found?" asked Jenny. "Couldn't they find out anything more about that?"

"No, that seems to be a dead end, too. Mrs. Henley, the woman who runs the house, denied knowing it was there and said nobody ever used that room next to Miss Bird's. And the police haven't been able to prove otherwise."

"If it was me, I'd go ahead and arrest her and see if that didn't make her talk," observed Susan. "It surprises me they don't arrest her anyway. She runs a house of ill-repute, or the next thing to it."

"That is true," I agreed. "And in fact Inspector Harper argued for doing just that. But his colleague, Inspector Freemantle, argued against it. He thinks leaving her free and keeping a watch on her place is more likely to pay off. 'If we give her enough rope, she'll hang herself,' is how he likes to put it. But nobody's been hanged yet or is likely to be, at the rate they're going."

Susan cleared her throat. "Seeing that's the case," she said, "you're going to have a bit of a dilemma on your hands. The Toths are scheduled for a sitting tomorrow night."

I was aware of it, Dear Reader. The idea of entertaining Absalom Toth again in my home was not pleasant. "I could put them off, I suppose," I said.

"Maybe you should," agreed Susan. "At least till you've talked with the Inspector."

These words made me bristle, though in fact I had been thinking along the same lines. "I don't need *his* permission," I said. "Or anyone's, in fact. As Mr. Toth is still a free man, I suppose I am free to have him here if I wish."

Susan preserved a discouraging silence. Jenny, however, clapped her hands in sudden inspiration. "I know," she said. "Maybe you can trap him, ma'am! Get him to confess it was him did the murders."

"No," said Susan with a groan. Turning an imploring look on me, she said, "For heaven's sake, let's not try *that* again! If it worked before, it was only purest luck that it did. And there's no saying but your luck might be out this time."

I tended to be of her opinion, Dear Reader, and yet there was a fascination in the idea. "I wonder," I said. "We *might* try something of the sort. Something that would surprise Mr. Toth into betraying himself."

"Very likely it wouldn't, though, and then where will you be? Far better to leave all that to the police."

"They're not having much luck at present," I said. "It might be time to try unconventional methods."

Seeing that her discouragements weren't working, Susan changed tactics. "It's not to be expected that Mrs. Toth will stand for you accusing her son of murder," she warned me. "If she doesn't know yet you're the one who told Scotland Yard about him, she will once you bring the Spirits into it. Then the whole business is bound to come out. And that'll be the end of her as a client—assuming her son doesn't pull out a knife at the séance table and put an end to *you*."

"I plan to take precautions against that," I said, reaching down to pat the revolver lying atop my right thigh. "The difficulty will be finding a way to shock Mr. Toth into confessing."

"How will you do it, ma'am?" asked Jenny eagerly. "How will you make him confess?"

"Susan mentioned a knife at the séance table," I said. "And that idea has definite possibilities. Not just a knife but a *bloody* knife. I wonder if that wouldn't be the way to proceed? Confront him with it and observe his reaction."

Susan rolled her eyes. Signora Mazzara couldn't have done it more dramatically, Dear Reader. "Will you listen to yourself?" she said. "It's not enough that he might have a knife with him, but you're going to give him one yourself?"

I told her we would grind the edge off the knife first. "It's only to use as a stage prop. Anyway, it wouldn't be very safe for us to be handling a sharp-edged knife in the dark."

"Us," said Susan. "*Us.* You're thinking I'm going to be a party to this folly?"

"Yes," I said. "If you're the woman I think you are, then yes, I do."

She was silenced, Dear Reader. Jenny observed wistfully that she wouldn't mind taking a hand, too. "And so you shall," I said. "It was your idea, after all. You can be in the next room with Susan, in case Mr. Toth cuts up ugly and we have to subdue him."

Susan muttered something inaudible. "I beg your pardon?" I said, addressing her politely. "Did you speak?"

"No," she said. "I was just saying to myself, you'd think somebody that'd survived one throat cutting wouldn't be so eager to court another. But who am I to argue if you want to put your neck in a noose?"

I opened my mouth to point out that she was mixing her metaphors, then realized it probably wasn't the best moment for a grammar lesson. "You are my trusted partner and associate," I told her. "And of course I value your opinion. And ordinarily I would agree with you about taking unnecessary risks. But in this case, I feel the risk might be worth it, if we can help solve this case."

"Ah, yes," said Susan. "There's a reward, isn't there, for information that helps catch the murderer?"

I admitted that there was a reward but told her I considered it beside the point. "I regard this as *pro bono publico* work. The murderer needs to be stopped by whatever means necessary. Even Felicity spoke about taking a hand—though to be sure, she has an interest that goes beyond the purely public. I gather all those extra policemen on the streets are inconveniencing her in her activities."

"I'll wager they are," said Susan, grinning in spite of herself. "Very well, ma'am. We've got till tomorrow night to get our plans worked out. I don't imagine that'll be any too much time, seeing we're hoping to do what Scotland Yard hasn't managed to do in the past six months."

Chapter 12

As I took my place with the Toths around the table that evening, I found myself wondering if Susan might have had a point after all.

It is always a touchy business to produce physical manifestations during a séance. That is the reason I invented the Spiritograph in the first place: to minimize the risks of my profession. In an earlier era, a Medium might extinguish all the lights and run around in the dark tapping people on the shoulder or shaking a tambourine and feel confident her clients would accept it as a genuine Spiritual experience. But nowadays people are far less naïve—though still credulous enough, if approached in the right way.

I only hoped I had chosen the right way that evening.

Mrs. Toth, across from me, was chattering away in her usual style. "Dear Madame Fox," she told me, "I have so been anticipating the chance to speak again with my Spiritual Spouse. All week I have sensed him trying to communicate with me in little ways. You remember, children, how the H volume of the encyclopædia fell onto the floor two nights ago? And when Ernestine spilled the salt at dinner last night, it very distinctly formed the shape of the letter T."

Miss Toth and Mr. Toth nodded dutifully. One might have supposed them a pair of puppets, responding simultaneously to a jerk of the string.

Looking at them now, it struck me how absurdly alike they were, in spite of the difference in sex. They both had pale faces with light-coloured, lashless eyes; they both had the same pinched features and colourless hair. It was true that Miss Toth wore hers in a skimpy knot atop her head and was clad in a shapeless greeny-yellow dress rather than trousers and a frock coat, but still the resemblance was striking.

"I feel this will be an exceptionally productive sitting," continued Mrs. Toth, her skeletal face alight with enthusiasm. "There is something in the air tonight that promises to be of unusual portent. I am sensitive to these things, you know. Indeed, I have been told I have Mediumistic abilities myself."

She sent a sharp look in my direction, whereupon I, too, responded dutifully. "Of course," I said. "There can be no doubt of it, ma'am. We would never get the results we get with the Spiritograph if it were only I who was mediating the Spirit Energy."

I had been nervous about meeting her tonight because I was uncertain whether she knew her son was suspected of being the New Moon Murderer—for which suspicion I was, of course, responsible. But it was obvious from her behaviour that she must be completely ignorant on both points.

I reminded myself that Mr. Toth clearly had lots of experience in keeping secrets from his mother. He, too, seemed quite as usual—almost alarmingly so. Considering that we were hoping to surprise him into a confession of guilt, I did not like to see him looking so limp and guileless. It seemed inconceivable that he could have even tried to kiss me, let alone commit the enormities we suspected him of. I told myself it only went to show how cleverly he was able to hide his true nature. But I could not feel it boded well for our plans tonight.

Meanwhile, Mrs. Toth was still chattering about her dear Henry. "I have seldom felt him so impatient to communicate," she declared. "It's clear he has something of unusual import to tell us tonight."

Indeed he did, Dear Reader, or rather *someone* did. I had not liked to saddle Mr. Thoreau with this particular errand. As mentioned before, a Medium comes to cherish proprietary feelings for her Spirits. This was such an ugly business—a world apart from Mr. Thoreau's wholesome pine forests and sparkling waters—that I planned to let an anonymous Spirit deliver the message and keep him uncontaminated.

I had another, more material reason for doing so, of course. If by some miracle I was able to retain Mrs. Toth as a client, it was altogether better that her Spiritual Spouse should have no connection with *this* business.

"Let us begin," I said.

I extinguished the lamps in the Spirit Parlour one by one, until only the candle was left burning in the hanging lantern above our heads.

"Let us join hands," I said.

Mr. Toth reached out to take my left hand in his right. I tried not to look as though I suspected it might be the hand of a murderer. Surreptitiously, I removed my revolver from its holster beneath my skirt and placed it in my lap before taking Miss Toth's left hand in my right.

"Let us concentrate," I said. "Shutting our eyes and relaxing our Earthly bodies, let us summon the Spirit Energy. Let us summon it so it surrounds and fills us."

The Toths were all used to this routine and shut their eyes obediently. I watched them from beneath my lashes. Time passed; the candle flickered, and then flickered again with a faint sizzling sound. I glanced at it with concern. Normally I leave the candle alight throughout the sitting, but on this occasion we needed complete darkness. I had planned for this by using a stump of a candle that would burn itself out without any action of mine. But I did not want it to burn out as early as this. A little delay is helpful in putting one's audience in the proper frame of mind to appreciate Spiritual phenomena.

Fortunately, the candle continued to burn for more or less the half-hour I had calculated upon. During this time, I could see the Toths growing restless. Normally Henry does not wait so long to manifest himself. Mrs. Toth in particular kept looking at me, her lips opening and closing as if she were about to speak. Finally she did speak, in an impatient undertone. "Is something amiss, Madame Fox? Is Henry not here yet?"

I shook my head, feigning an expression of concern. "I feel him, but I feel also the presence of another Spirit," I told her. "We must shut our eyes and concentrate harder."

Scarcely had I spoken than the candle flared, dimmed, and went out with a little pop. There were gasps from the Toths. "Do not break the circle," I warned them. As I spoke, I tightened my grip on Mr. and Miss Toth's hands—on Mr. Toth's especially. It was vital that I not lose track of him in the dark. If he gave any sign of reaching for a hidden knife, I wanted to have warning enough to take measures.

"There is a Spirit present," I announced.

The Spiritograph chimed in agreement.

"Is this the Spirit of Henry David Thoreau?" I asked.

Only silence greeted the question.

"Is this another Spirit?"

The bell rang.

"Do you have a message for someone in this room?"

Again the bell rang.

"What is the message?"

A long silence followed, in which we could feel the air stirring around us. It felt very eerie in the pitch-black room. A ghostly presence seemed to approach the table and then recede. More silence followed, and then a sigh, and after that a strange, faraway whisper from somewhere above our heads, the words unintelligible.

I waited a few minutes, giving Susan time to gather up her equipment and withdraw into the next room. Then I spoke again. "I feel the Spirit Energy fading," I said. "The Spirit is departing."

"But Henry?" inquired Mrs. Toth's voice from the darkness. "What about Henry?"

I spoke again in my Medium's voice: "If there is still a Spirit present, let us know."

Only silence greeted the request. I repeated it twice more, then let out a sigh of my own. "Nothing," I said. "The Energy appears to have been depleted by the first Spirit."

"How very strange," said Mrs. Toth, in a tone that clearly meant *how very unsatisfactory.*

I agreed it was very strange. "I fear we will get no further result tonight," I said with another theatrical sigh. "I may as well relight the lamps."

As soon as I released Mr. Toth's hand, I quickly distanced myself from him in the darkness. Then, moving cautiously around the table, I came to a halt at a point that I reckoned to be directly behind his mother's chair. From there, I took a series of careful steps backwards, until I felt my skirt brush the plinth of one of the statues that lined the wall. I placed my revolver carefully on the plinth, then pulled a box of vestas from my pocket, struck one, and lit the nearest oil lamp.

The lamplight was painfully bright to eyes accustomed to darkness. I could see the Toths blinking as their vision adjusted. It took a little time for them to notice the knife lying artistically in front of them in a little pool of blood. It was in fact beef blood, obtained from our local butcher, but the effect was quite as striking as if it had been human.

"What?" demanded Mrs. Toth, her voice apoplectic. "*What* is the meaning of this?"

I kept my eyes on Mr. Toth, but he said nothing. His expression, as far as I could tell, was one of pure bewilderment. He sat looking at the knife without making any move to touch it. Nor did he make any move toward a hidden weapon of his own.

It was Miss Toth who moved, erupting from her chair like a quail from covert. She stood trembling for a moment, gazing down at the knife, then turned and stumbled across the room making strange bleating noises. I stared at her, dumfounded.

She reached the door of the Spirit Parlour and stood there, still trembling and bleating. "Ernestine," said her mother sharply. "Ernestine, are you unwell? Are you going to faint?"

Miss Toth looked at her, then at me. There was such a strong appeal in her eyes that I hurried toward her, supposing she was indeed about to faint.

Her legs buckled just as I reached her. Putting an arm around her, I eased her down to the floor. "Lie still," I said. "Shut your eyes and take deep breaths. I'll send for smelling salts."

When I would have departed on this errand, however, she reached out, grasped my sleeve, and pulled me towards her. "Don't tell Mother," she whispered. "I didn't mean to hurt you, Madame Fox. Truly I didn't. Please, please let me explain."

Chapter 13

It took a little time for me to get my wits together, Dear Reader. My mind was whirling as I went to summon Susan. Fortunately, she had observed Miss Toth's fit through the ventilator, and when I opened the Spirit Parlour door, she was standing there with smelling salts in hand and no need for summoning.

She had brought brandy as well, forgetting the Toths were teetotalers. Mrs. Toth reminded her of it sharply, and with an air of deep suspicion. You would have supposed Susan meant to pour hemlock down her daughter's throat. Susan took umbrage at this, naturally enough, but I drew her aside under the pretext of reprimanding her.

"Never mind the brandy," I whispered. "A glass of water will do. And find some excuse to get Mrs. Toth out of the room."

A flash of understanding glinted in her eye. "Very well, ma'am," she said.

It took several tries before we could get Mrs. Toth to leave the Spirit Parlour. Fortunately, Miss Toth helped us by resuming her seat at the table and adjusting her features to a semblance of normalcy. "It's all right, Mother," she said. "I will just sit here quietly for a moment and compose myself. No, you needn't stay. Indeed, I would rather be by myself."

By this time Susan had taken the knife away and wiped the table of blood, so that Miss Toth's desire to remain there did not seem extraordinary. Adjuring her to keep the smelling salts nearby in case she felt faint again, Mrs. Toth finally consented to leave her and go into the Sitting Room along with her son. I accompanied them there, then excused myself, ostensibly to fetch tea.

When I re-entered the Spirit Parlour, Miss Toth was sitting rigidly upright, her hands folded around the vinaigrette. Her eyes were shut, but she opened them as I entered and watched as I closed the door behind me. "Thank you," she whispered. "Thank you for not telling Mother."

"As to that," I said, "I am making no promises. This is an ugly business, Miss Toth. You owe me an explanation, at the very least."

She nodded, her face working. "I know," she said. "But I can't tell you now—not while Mother's here." She glanced nervously toward the door. "May I come back later? After Mother's in bed? Come back and explain?"

I hesitated, Dear Reader. If she was indeed the person who had held a knife to my throat a few weeks ago, then it seemed imprudent to allow her back into my house for a second try. On the other hand, I was eager to hear her explanation, and she appeared harmless enough at the moment. I reasoned I could have Sam and Jenny standing by to subdue her if she were moved to assault me again.

"Very well," I said. "I am willing to listen to your explanation. But do you think you can come back tonight without your mother knowing?"

"Oh, yes," she assured me. "Absalom often goes out at night without her knowing."

"So I gathered," I said, rather dryly. "Very well, Miss Toth. Wait here a moment or two, then come along to the Sitting Room and tell your mother you are well enough to go home. I'll go now to be with her and your brother."

***

After the Toths had left, I quickly acquainted Susan and Jenny with Miss Toth's admission of guilt. They were both astounded.

"It was *her*?" said Susan. "*She* was the one who attacked you?"

"So it seems. I suppose she might be lying again to protect her brother, but it didn't sound like it. And the evidence does seem to show he wouldn't have had time to come here that night." I gasped suddenly, as a piece of the puzzle fell into place. "That's it! Not only did she come here that night, *she* was the second man!"

I could tell from Susan's expression that she shared my epiphany, but Jenny looked confused. "Second man?" she repeated.

"The man Inspector Freemantle saw on the night of the last New Moon. He and another policeman were secretly following Mr. Toth that night. They saw him meet this other man who was about his height and build and dressed much like him. In fact, they looked so much alike that the police couldn't tell them apart. So when the two men eventually split up, they had to follow both of them. But the constable who was deputed to follow Mr. Toth lost him." I thought this over, trying to see if there was any flaw in the Miss-Toth-as-Second-Man theory. I couldn't see that there was, but Jenny had an objection.

"But Miss Toth is a lady," she said. "And the inspector said it was a *man* with Mr. Toth."

"Yes," I said. "But Miss Toth and her brother look amazingly alike. I was noticing it just tonight, before the séance. Miss Toth is quite as tall as he is and practically as flat-chested. If she were wearing pantaloons and had her hair tucked under a man's hat, I daresay she would look just like him." I gasped again as another piece of puzzle slipped into place. "And she would be used to wearing pantaloons, too, for the Toths espouse dress reform. I remember Mrs. Toth saying that years ago they had actually lived in an Owenite community where all the women wore pantaloons."

"But they wear dresses here in London," pointed out Jenny.

"If you can *call* them dresses," said Susan with a sniff. "Shapeless things that look like nothing on earth."

I explained that Miss Toth's shapeless dresses also fell under the category of dress reform. "You'd find them much more comfortable than your own dresses, Susan," I added mischievously. "No need for corsets."

"I notice *you* wear corsets," she shot back.

"In my position, I can't afford to ignore Fashion," I said. "But between you and me, I'm always glad to take them off."

Jenny got the conversation back on track by inquiring if I thought it was safe to let Miss Toth into the house again. "I think so," I said. "Now that we know it was she who attacked me the other night, she would be mad to try it again."

"Perhaps she *is* mad," said Susan. "Have you thought of that?"

I told her I *had* thought of it, surreptitiously touching my revolver once more. I had replaced it in its hidden holster during the confusion following Miss Toth's fit. "But I believe there's something behind all this, and I want badly to know what it is. It might help Inspector Harper solve the case."

At that moment, the doorbell rang. Susan, muttering something about curiosity and cats, got up to answer it. She returned a moment later with Miss Toth, who entered the Sitting Room with a hesitating step, as though proceeding to the guillotine.

Behind her back, Susan mimed a gesture of scribbling on paper, then raised her eyebrows. I nodded, whereupon she withdrew from the Sitting Room leaving the door slightly ajar. I gave her time to provide herself with paper and pencil, then urged Miss Toth to take a seat. "And I think you would be the better for a little brandy," I said, pouring a few ounces of the spirit into a glass and handing it to her. "I know you and your family are teetotalers, but you have had a shock, and I think you could use some stimulant."

A faint flush appeared on Miss Toth's face. "It's Mother who is the teetotaler," she said. "Absalom and I never had any choice in the matter. For my part, I should quite *like* to have some brandy."

Despite her brave words, she hesitated before taking a sip from the glass. "But how nasty," she exclaimed, sounding much surprised. "Why, I supposed liquor would taste *good*. It's supposed to be wicked, isn't it? But I can't see why anyone would *want* to drink such nasty stuff."

I advised her to keep sipping at it and she might find out. "Meanwhile, perhaps you can tell me why you thought it was a good idea to come here the other night and threaten to cut my throat."

Miss Toth shrank a little at these words, but already the brandy was having a strengthening effect. "It was a foolish thing to do," she admitted after a bit. "A *wicked* thing to do. If I hadn't been so upset with you, I never would have done it."

"But why were you upset with me?"

She looked at me with surprise. "Because of Absalom," she said. "I thought you knew. I thought the Spirits would have told you."

I explained quickly that the Spirits had been rather vague. "I don't understand why you had a grudge against me on your brother's account."

"Because you told the police he was a murderer," she said. "The one who's been killing all those women." There was a touch of consternation in her voice as she added, "It *was* you, wasn't it? Absalom thought it must be, because of *Walden*. And because someone told us you had helped the police before in their cases."

Although I had tried to keep this fact a secret, Dear Reader, I was not surprised to hear it had leaked out. Inspector Harper and I had worked together on several prominent cases in which a great many people had been involved. It was no wonder if a few of them had talked. Besides, anyone who cared to watch might have seen him visiting me and the Temple on a regular basis.

"It was, in fact, I who suggested your brother might have left *Walden* at the scene of Matilda Bird's murder," I acknowledged. "The police inspector investigating the case asked me about it, and I felt it my duty to tell him what I knew."

"You had no right to do that!" charged Miss Toth. "Absalom had nothing to do with those murders."

"He had been in that room, and known Miss Bird," I pointed out. "Known her rather well, as it appears."

A faint flush appeared on Miss Toth's cheeks once more. "Yes, I know," she said. After a moment's pause, she added, "But he didn't kill her."

"But surely you understand the police have to investigate every lead? That they must do everything possible to stop the person responsible for killing those women?"

"I don't care about those women," she shot back. "They were bad women—wicked. It's Absalom I care about."

"Even if he's the one who's killing them?"

"He's not," she said earnestly. "I *know* he's not. He couldn't do such a thing."

The expression on my face must have shown her this was hardly a convincing argument. She went on, stumbling for words. "He might have—might have *been* with Miss Bird. In fact, I know he *was* with her. And—and with other women of that sort—"

"Wicked," I supplied, dryly.

"Yes, wicked," she agreed, quite in earnest. She fixed me with her strange pale eyes. "They *are* wicked, you know—those women. One of them gave Absalom a disease. A *nasty* disease." Her face twisted with distaste.

I felt almost as though I were talking to Inspector Freemantle again. "I daresay," I said. "But I cannot see that anything compelled him to seek out women of that sort, or to indulge in conduct that would result in his getting a disease from them."

Miss Toth could not be brought to admit this. "Women of that sort are always trying to snare men into wickedness," she insisted. "And Absalom—well, Absalom is weak in that way. I know that he is. The doctors told Mother he has appetitive and phrenetic tendencies."

"Doctors?" I repeated.

"At the asylum," she explained. Once again she fixed me with her strange pale gaze. "That's why I was so angry about your talking to the police. I know Absalom didn't commit those murders, and the police won't be able to prove he did. But if Mother finds out he's been with women of that sort, she'll send him back to the asylum."

I drew the whole story out of her eventually, Dear Reader. It appeared that even as a small boy, Mr. Toth had been preoccupied with sexual matters to an unnatural degree—or, at any rate, to what his mother considered an unnatural degree. And so, in an effort to cure him, she had consigned him to a lunatic asylum. His first stay had been of several years' duration, at a time when he was not yet in his teens. His offense back then had been what Miss Toth euphemistically called self-abuse, but more latterly his offenses had involved women.

"The last time, it was during his medical training," said Miss Toth in a voice barely above a whisper. "He was studying to be an eclectic doctor. And there was rather an unfortunate incident involving one of his lady patients."

I could imagine that there was, Dear Reader. Probably she had smiled at him. Of course I felt sorry for the lady patient, but I found myself a little sorry for Mr. Toth, too. It was not surprising that he had grown twisted, after being sent as a child to a mental institution for behaviour so wholly natural. There are, to be sure, plenty of doctors who will tell you masturbation is dangerous, but you will also find plenty of doctors who say women lack sexual feelings. And if you believe *that*, Dear Reader, you have been reading this narrative to no purpose. It's all medical quackery, in my opinion.

"I can see you would want to protect your brother," I said, choosing my words carefully, "but even if you are right and he hasn't committed these murders, it seems to me he has behaved recklessly—so recklessly that it almost amounts to insanity. Going out at night and consorting with prostitutes when he knows that a word from your mother would send him back into an institution."

Miss Toth nodded, looking worried. "He *is* reckless," she said. "I have tried to convince him not to go out, but he won't listen to me. Even after that business with Miss Bird, and the police questioning him." Her eyes filled with tears. "You can't think what a near thing that was. The police coming and asking to speak with him—and of course Mother had to know what it was about. He made up a story about his watch being stolen, which satisfied her for a time. But then they came and questioned him again after this last murder. He said it was about his watch again, but I think she suspects. If she doesn't, she soon will, if the police keep coming and wanting to talk with him."

I didn't have much comfort to offer her, Dear Reader. I wasn't sure she deserved comfort in any case. "You claim your brother did not commit the murders," I said. "But somebody did, and it was somebody who knew Miss Bird. Knew of her, at least, and knew she was a prostitute."

She agreed that this was true, in a voice that did not seem to grasp the significance of my words. I went on, watching her closely. "And this last murder—Lizzie Gowd, the woman who was found dead in the churchyard. Your brother had walked by that same churchyard on the night she was murdered."

She nodded. "Yes," she said. "That's what Absalom said. But he didn't know it till the police told him."

"Don't you think that's rather a coincidence?"

She considered the question solemnly, as if it were a purely theoretical matter. "I suppose it *is* a coincidence, rather," she said. "Though I'd be more inclined to call it bad luck myself."

"And don't you think it's also rather a coincidence that you came here that same night and threatened to cut my throat?"

She had caught the drift of my questions now, Dear Reader. She looked a little frightened. "But I wasn't going to," she said. "I just hoped it would keep you from talking to the police any more."

"How could you possibly think it would do that?" I demanded. "It was much more likely to make me run straight to them and tell them the whole story—as in fact I did."

She bit her lip. "Yes . . . yes, of course. Very well, then. Perhaps I *did* think of cutting your throat." She looked at me defiantly. "If I had, you wouldn't have been able to talk to the police any more. Not only that, but when they investigated your murder, they would have known it couldn't have been Absalom who did it. So I borrowed some of his clothes and took one of the kitchen knives and slipped out of the house after he had gone. I came here and hid in your bedroom and waited till you came in. And when you did, I meant to kill you. But once I had the knife to your throat, I couldn't do it. It hadn't been real till then, you see."

I thought I did see, Dear Reader, although it made the hair rise on the back of my neck to think what a narrow escape I had had. "You don't think it was my screaming that made you change your mind?" I asked, with just the slightest touch of irony.

"No, for I had already decided not to kill you when you started screaming," she assured me seriously. "I was standing there, trying to think what to do and how to get away without being caught. And then when you screamed, I stopped thinking at all and just ran. And when I had got a little way down the street, I realized it had worked out splendidly. You'd tell the police about my being there, of course, but when they investigated, they would know it couldn't have been Absalom. And I didn't think they would ever guess it might have been me."

"I think they might have got on your trail eventually," I said, watching her closely once again. "They saw you with your brother that night, you see."

"Saw me?" she said, looking puzzled. "With Absalom?"

"Yes," I said. "Near the churchyard where Miss Gowd was murdered. He was being followed by two policemen at the time."

Her reaction struck me as rather obtuse. "Then that shows he couldn't have murdered Miss Gowd," she said triumphantly. "Not if the police were watching him."

"But it shows you might have," I pointed out. "They weren't watching *you.*"

She stared at me, her brow furrowed. "But I wasn't there," she said. "I never saw Absalom that night—not after he left the house."

"You told the police you were together all evening."

She hung her head. "Yes, I did. That was a lie, of course. I didn't know then that he was . . . with someone."

"With a woman," I said, watching her.

"Yes," she agreed ruefully. "With a woman. It made me look a great fool, and Absalom was no end upset with me. Of course we really weren't together that evening. I just said we were, thinking it would be an alibi for him. And for me, too, of course."

"But you *were* with him," I said. "The policemen who were following your brother saw you join him, walk together for a way, and then separate. It must have been shortly after you left here."

The expression on her face looked like genuine astonishment, Dear Reader. "That couldn't have been I," she said. "I went straight home after leaving here. And I never saw Absalom at all that night."

I was out of charity with her already over the matter of the throat cutting, and this made me lose my patience completely. "You may as well admit it," I snapped. "There's no point in lying now."

"But I'm not lying," she protested. "Why do you say I am?"

"Because you have *already* lied to me, *and* to the police," I said. "What do you think you have to gain by concealing anything now?"

"But I'm not! I'm not concealing anything. Not now." Once more her eyes filled with tears. "I know I have been wicked—very wicked indeed. I am willing to tell the police the truth now, even if it means I must go to jail. But it wasn't I they saw with Absalom that night. I don't know who it was, but it wasn't I."

Chapter 14

"You should have called me immediately," said Inspector Harper severely. "What were you thinking of, to confront the woman yourself?"

I had sent a note round to him the next morning, Dear Reader: the morning after my conversation with Miss Toth. It had been so late when we had finished, and Miss Toth so utterly demoralized, that I had decided to postpone any further action until the following day.

In part, this was because I wasn't sure what action was called for. I still felt Miss Toth was lying about not meeting her brother on the night of Miss Gowd's murder. She had, after all, lied initially about her intent to murder *me*. And after that revelation, I felt I owed her no further consideration. The proper thing to do would be to put her immediately in the hands of the police.

Yet even knowing this, I had not done it. I supposed I had got in the habit of feeling sorry for her and her brother. At any rate, I had allowed her to go home after telling her that she must make herself available to the police whenever they wanted her. She had agreed meekly to this condition, but now, as I sat watching Inspector Harper read through the transcript of our conversation, it struck me that I had been foolishly trusting.

He was good enough not to say so, at least. "An extraordinary business," he commented, laying aside the transcript. "Who would have supposed she was at the bottom of it?"

"Do you think she was?"

He seemed startled by my question. "It seems pretty clear," he said. "As you noted yourself, she lied about that other business. It wasn't until she was caught in the lie that she confessed. And she admitted quite frankly that she came here that night to murder you. No, I can't think of any other explanation that fits the facts."

"It does fit the facts very neatly," I agreed. I had been struck by this point myself, Dear Reader. I found myself dwelling on it now, trying to convince myself we had got to the bottom of the business.

Inspector Harper, who knows me well, had caught something in the tone of my voice. "But you're not convinced," he said, making the words a statement rather than a question. "Why not?"

I could only shake my head. "Because I am a fool, I suppose. Her story is damning enough in all conscience. Indeed, I have been calling myself a fool all night, wondering why I simply didn't send for you straightway and put her in your hands. If she's decamped in the night and taken the first boat home to the States, it would serve me right."

He nodded, regarding me with a thoughtful air. "But you're *not* a fool," he said. "In general, you have pretty good instincts about these things. I'd be interested to know why you don't think Miss Toth is guilty."

"I'm not sure I can put it in words, Tom. Besides, does it matter? If the evidence shows she's guilty, then there's nothing more to be said."

"In theory that ought to be true," he agreed. "But interpreting evidence is a delicate business. That's where Ned Freemantle goes astray, in my opinion. If he finds a piece of evidence that doesn't fit his theory, he either twists it until it does or discards it altogether. It's a great mistake to put theory ahead of facts, I've always found."

"But I don't *have* any facts," I said.

"Maybe you do and don't know it. At any rate, I'd be glad of your opinion."

I thought carefully, trying to analyze why I felt Miss Toth was not the murderer. "I think it's because her reactions weren't right," I said at last. "When I told her she would have to tell the police everything she had told me, she seemed more concerned about her mother finding out than what the police might do to her."

"And if she were going to be arrested for murder, her mother's reaction ought to be the least of her worries," he said with a nod. "Yes, that's a point, to be sure."

Hearing it put into words made me want to argue the other side of the case, Dear Reader. "But you're assuming we're talking about a normal person here," I said. "And the Toths are anything but normal. If you saw the way Ernestine and Absalom Toth cringe before their mother! It's obvious they're more afraid of her than anything else in the world."

"Not surprising, if she holds the threat of an asylum over their heads," said Inspector Harper.

"I'm coming to think that's the best place for them both," I said frankly. "After listening to Miss Toth last night, I'd say she's as mad as her brother."

He said the facts might well support such a conclusion. "That would mean Broadmoor[14] if she's convicted," he said. "They're not likely to hang a woman, however guilty she might be. And of course she *is* guilty, of the attack on you if nothing else. Do you want to prefer charges?"

I considered this question at length, Dear Reader. On one hand, I still felt resentful toward Miss Toth. She had come to my home with the fixed intention of killing me—an offense that certainly deserved punishment. On the other hand, it would do me no good, either personally or professionally, to be publicly tied with this case. Even if Miss Toth were never convicted of the other murders, I would find myself lumped together with the other victims as a putative prostitute.

At bottom, however, it was pity that turned the scale. Much as I might long to punish her, I was inclined to think being Ernestine Toth was punishment enough.

"No," I said finally. "No, I don't wish to prefer charges."

He nodded, looking resigned. "I can't say I blame you. It's not a business I'd want to have you mixed up in, speaking from a purely personal point of view. Speaking as a policeman, however, I'm afraid it will make it harder for us to fix her guilt. The attack on you is the only crime she has admitted to."

---

[14] Broadmoor Criminal Lunatic Asylum—*Ed.*

I told him that he could always tell Miss Toth I meant to prosecute, if it would help him in his inquiries. He thanked me, saying he would hold the threat as a weapon in reserve. "But we might not need it, if we can get evidence she murdered those other women. We've not investigated her at all at this point, beyond determining that she was lying about her brother being home on the night of the last New Moon."

"I wonder what Inspector Freemantle will make of this new development?" I speculated.

"At first glance, it doesn't seem to support his theory," said Inspector Harper, smiling. "But Miss Toth did talk a lot about wickedness, didn't she? She might well have seen herself as an instrument in the Lord's hands, tasked with striking down the wicked scarlet women." He shook his head ruefully. "I daresay Ned could do a lot with that."

He got up to leave at this point, and I escorted him to the door. "I suppose you must call on Miss Toth now, to get a statement," I said. "I wonder how she will explain *that* to her mother? I'm afraid the device of the stolen watch is going to seem a bit threadbare at this point."

He smiled kindly. "We'll be as discreet as possible. As I say, we don't go out of our way to make trouble for people. Until we can prove her guilt, she's innocent in the eyes of the law." His jaw tightened. "But I hope at least we find enough to justify putting her under lock and key. The dark of the moon is coming up again, and the last thing we need is another one of these murders."

***

For the next few days I watched the newspapers for word of Miss Toth's arrest. There was no mention of it, however, so I was forced to assume the police had not yet found evidence that would prove her guilt—if indeed she *were* guilty. Susan and Jenny and I argued the point at length, but without reaching any definite conclusion.

I tried to distract myself with other matters, chief among them being *Night and Day*. The date of opening night was rapidly approaching, and the opera house was buzzing like an overturned hive in anticipation. The scenery was mostly done, and so were the costumes, and I was amused to see that I had been quite right about Signora Mazzara making sure she was not outshone by her younger cast-mate. When I arrived at the theatre that afternoon, I found the signora resplendent in star-spangled black chiffon, very clinging and décolleté, while Miss Dart was enveloped in dark grey flowing robes that largely concealed both her face and figure.

Both women were seated in the pit, watching Signor Adriano (Apollo) perform his aria, "Deeds of Darkness." I had heard it before, but not with full orchestration. Mr. Witters had used double basses and kettledrums to underline the sinister nature of the action onstage, and the theatre reverberated with their low-pitched throbbing as I slipped into a seat beside the signora.

She flashed me a smile of welcome, then turned her attention back to the stage. "It is very good," she said, in a calm, detached voice. "Nino is most excellent. I find myself sorry the part of Lucien was not scored for baritone so we could sing together. Such fire, such passion he brings to his rôles!"

I told her I thought Mr. Cardle made a fine Lucien, at which she shook her head sadly. "You English are so cold," she complained. "Mr. Cardle is better than most, but it is not the same." She gestured toward Signor Adriano. "He will steal the show from poor Mr. Cardle. See if I am not right. You English are so cold!"

I overlooked the insult to my country, Dear Reader. In fact, I am American by birth, not English, though I pass as an Englishwoman over here. "I suppose it is not usual for a baritone to sing the leading male rôle?" I asked.

"Not usual, but there are some," she said. "Figaro, of course, and Don Giovanni. But Mr. Witters, he would never think of *that*," she added scathingly.

I was sorry I had not known this before, Dear Reader. If I had, I might have stipulated a baritone for the part of Lucien. I do prefer voices in the lower range, both male and female. I would guess Inspector Harper, for instance, has a baritone voice.

I amused myself by casting him and the other Scotland Yard officers in operatic rôles. The Chief Commissioner would undoubtedly be a bass, in keeping with the gravitas of his office. And of course Detective Inspector Freemantle, the Yard's up-and-coming young star, would be leading tenor. Nothing else would satisfy him, I was sure.

At this point, the signora's voice broke in on my thoughts. "Ah, but that fool of a second violinist has come in early once again," she hissed. "Pig! Dog! *Malledetto bastardo*!"

She half-rose from her seat, but the orchestra leader had already taken the erring violinist to task. The rehearsal resumed a moment later, and once again "Deeds of Darkness" filled the air.

It struck me as a pretty pervasive theme, both inside and outside the theatre. I found my mind wandering to the Toths now as I reflected on the question of the second man. It was hard to know whether Miss Toth was telling the truth about that when she had lied about so many other things. Evidently the police had failed to establish her guilt, but perhaps they still had hopes of doing so.

For my part, I hoped Inspector Harper would find a moment to call on me soon and tell me how the investigation was going. It would be pleasant if he had time for a personal visit as well. But with the dark of the moon approaching, I knew he would be busy patrolling the streets with the other policemen. I thought it unlikely there would be another murder if either of the Toths were the guilty party, but it wasn't impossible. They were such odd, unaccountable folk that I hesitated to say what they might not do. Still, the police would undoubtedly take extra precautions to see they were followed this time, assuming they were mad enough to go out that night.

I was glad when the dancers came onstage to rehearse the "Moonlight" ballet. Their pretty antics made a pleasant change from Deeds of Darkness. Mr. Hinney came and sat beside me, and we watched the ballet together while the signora and Miss Dart went backstage for a costume fitting.

"It's going well," he told me. "Of course, our Lucien is down with a bilious fit which he's pleased to call a heart attack. God only knows whether he'll be able to sing on opening night. And the scene painters tell me the last of the sets won't be ready until then—*if* we're lucky enough to have them done at all. And Paola's got her understudy so cowed that the poor girl hardly dares open her mouth to rehearse, so God knows what will happen if *she* falls ill. But I'd say it's going well, on the whole."

"Would you?" I asked, amazed to hear this catalog of woes so easily discounted.

His eyes twinkled at me. "Certainly I would. In this business, there's always something to worry about. But I expect it will go well enough on the night, one way or another."

It was cheering to spend time in the company of someone so sanguine, Dear Reader. I ended up staying long enough to watch the signora sing "Do You Not Dream?" and hit the high A without difficulty before excusing myself to return home.

As usual, I had Sam stop at the newsstand on the corner so I might purchase the evening papers. As I went to pay for them, the headline on the *London Banner* caught my eye. I stopped short, staring at it. "POSSIBLE SUSPECT IN NEW MOON MURDERS," it read, and in the smaller print below I could just distinguish the name Absalom Toth.

Chapter 15

I skimmed the article hastily in the carriage, then read it carefully once I got home. Finally, I called in Susan and Jenny, and we all read it together.

"So the police think it was Mr. Toth after all?" said Susan incredulously. "Not Miss Toth?"

"It could be," said Jenny, looking to me for support. "Couldn't it, ma'am? The Inspector said Mr. Toth had got an alibi for the night of the last New Moon, but the victim in that case might have been killed earlier or later."

"Quite right," I said. "That must be the line they're taking. They think Mr. Toth killed Miss Gowd sometime other than the night of the New Moon. During the previous day or night, probably. The police were busy questioning him the next day, so he likely wouldn't have had a chance then, even if he was willing to take the risk."

"And so they've arrested him," said Susan, still sounding incredulous.

"It doesn't actually say they've arrested him," I pointed out. "Only that he's suspected."

"But it must be they're going to," said Susan. "Surely they wouldn't put it in the newspaper otherwise?"

I hesitated a little before answering that. "They might," I said. "It's the *Banner*, after all. They print all sorts of rubbish."

"Like that lampoon about *you*," said Susan acutely.

I contented myself with saying that I wouldn't hang a dog on the *Banner's* recommendation. "But there must be something behind it—on this occasion, anyway. The police may have found new evidence, or even got Mr. Toth to confess."

It was all I could do not to send for Inspector Harper straightway. But a glance at the clock showed me it was almost time for my evening sitting. I got through it somehow and through the rest of the evening as well, wondering all the while what lay behind the newspaper's words.

***

Fortunately, I wasn't kept in suspense for very long. I was eating breakfast in the Sitting Room the next morning when Susan came in to say that Inspector Harper was at the door. I told her to lay another plate and show him in. He came into the room a little hesitantly, a rueful smile on his face. He had obviously just come off night patrol and was dressed as a sailor in a pea jacket and midshipman's cap.

I told him I was charmed to see this unexpected side of him. "Of course all the services have their appeal to womanly hearts," I said. "But the Navy has perhaps the most romantic associations of all. One thinks of dear Miss Austen, and *Persuasion*, and the domestic virtues of Captain Wentworth and his fellow sailing men."

He smiled and ran a hand over his unshaven cheek. "I would beg your pardon for appearing this way," he said. "But you understand how it is. I'm just off duty and wanted to let you know about this latest development. You've seen the *Banner?"*

I told him I had. "So Absalom Toth is under arrest?"

He took a little time to answer that, stirring sugar into his tea and helping himself to ham before he spoke. "I expect he's under arrest by now. For his own protection, if nothing else. After that article appeared, there was a mob crying for his blood. It wouldn't be safe for him to show his face in public at this point."

I said the article had certainly implied he was a dangerous character. "Have you found new evidence to prove his guilt?"

The Inspector shook his head. "Not really. The article forced our hand. The whole city's on edge about these murders. We could hardly let the fellow go free, once word got out he might be the killer. But between you and me, I'll be surprised if we can hold him. Not unless we turn up something more than we've got."

I asked him if the police now supposed Miss Toth to be innocent.

"Yes," he said. "We've found nothing to link her to the other murders, and she seems to have solid alibis for at least some of them."

"Does she still deny being the second man?"

"Yes, she does. And her brother backs her up, for what that's worth."

"It wouldn't be worth very much, if he denies there was ever a second man at all," I said. "Has he changed his story about that?"

"No, he hasn't. But of course, that might just be brotherly chivalry, if it really was his sister that night."

"Do you think it was?"

He shook his head slowly. "I've spoken with Miss Toth myself," he said, "and I've come to share your opinion. I think she's innocent of everything except the attack on you. Ned shares that opinion, too. He was quite excited at first, thinking she might be the killer, but now he's inclined to think she's a red herring."

"And it's her brother who's the killer instead?"

He nodded, his expression reserved. "That's what Ned believes, anyway. As do quite a few others on the force."

"But you don't believe it yourself?"

He was silent a moment, considering. "I don't know if I believe it or not," he said, "but I don't like it. That article appearing when it did and forcing our hand—it's a strange, smoky business. I'd like to know who put the *Banner* onto Absalom Toth."

"You think it was someone at Scotland Yard?"

"I'd hate to think so," he said, "but it's possible. Journalists pay well for that kind of information. Now and then, we get a man on the force who's not above being bought."

He looked so unhappy at the idea that I sought to distract him. "I suppose the cat is out of the bag as far as Mrs. Toth is concerned," I said. "She knows now it's not a stolen watch that's got the police interested in her son."

He smiled a little at these words. "Yes, she knows," he said. "She knows, and I can tell you she's not happy about it. A most formidable woman."

I asked if she was trying to regulate Mr. Toth's jail diet. He laughed and said she was. "I had never heard of an aspiring vegetable before. Poor fellow, no wonder he looks half-starved. Perhaps a spell in jail will do him good. Although he does seem to partake of her ideas by and large."

"Not all of them," I said. "I'm sure it was a shock for her to learn about him and his mistresses."

He ran his hand through his hair. "She's flatly refused to believe he's capable of that sort of thing. But she'll have to accept it in the end. That part of the evidence is strong, and he's admitted himself that he and Miss Bird were on intimate terms."

"But not that he killed her," I said.

"No, there's no shaking him on that point. And the fact he left *Walden* there in her room is hardly evidence of his guilt. We've even less to tie him to Miss Gowd's murder, unless you count the fact he walked by the churchyard that night. And that's nothing like conclusive, either, for if he did murder her, he didn't do it then."

"Doesn't that upset Inspector Freemantle's theory?" I asked. "The fact that he would have had to murder her sometime other than the dark of the moon?"

"Oh, it turns out his theory is elastic enough to accommodate a day or two either way," said Inspector Harper with a short laugh. "But if Toth's the New Moon Murderer, he didn't deviate at all in his schedule until this last killing. I can't reconcile that with lunacy. It seems more like expediency to me."

I said it seemed that way to me, too, offering him more ham as I spoke. He was glad to accept my offer, remarking that it made a pleasant change from Mrs. McIntyre's sour bread and burnt porridge.

"That woman," I said. "She probably burns the porridge on purpose, out of spite."

"I've often wondered," he said, regarding me with a humourous eye. "But it's no matter. At least she doesn't restrict me to aspiring vegetables."

Since we were discussing personal matters at this point, I ventured to issue an invitation I had been hesitating over for the past week. "Would you care to attend opening night at the opera this Friday, Tom?" I asked. "I have a box for it."

He looked interested. "That's *your* opera? The one you helped write?"

I gave him a stern look. "The one *Signor Roberto Russo* wrote, via my mediation."

He said meekly that that was what he had meant. "I'd very much like to go, Seraphina. But I don't know . . . this murder business may interfere. You know if there's another killing, I'm liable to have my hands full."

"In that case," I said, "I hope Absalom Toth *is* the New Moon Murderer. Now that he's in jail, he won't be in a position to murder anyone over the next few days."

He said that would almost reconcile him to Ned Freemantle's being proved right. "I'll come if it's at all possible," he promised me. Reaching across the table, he took my hand in his. "Indeed, I'd be sorry to miss it. Quite a coup for you, isn't it?"

I told him the coup seemed in some doubt at this point. "We'll hope it comes off. But I would be glad to have your support in any case."

"Well, if I'm to cut any kind of figure as your escort, I'll have to provide myself with more fitting attire than this," he said, with a rueful look at his sailor's garb. More seriously, he added, "I do apologize for appearing before you in such a guise. I hope I haven't entirely disgusted you."

I said I was not disgusted at all and adduced convincing proofs of it, which made him say he could understand why tars were traditionally described as jolly, by Jove. But just when things looked in a promising way for a little post-prandial diversion, the doorbell rang. Knowing that Susan was busy below-stairs, I excused myself and went to answer it. I was a little vexed at the interruption, Dear Reader. If it were a client, I would be obliged to give him or her my attention, and then Inspector Harper would probably go home to the odious Mrs. McIntyre.

When I opened the door, however, I found a young man holding a pad of folded flannel to one side of his face. He wore an agonized expression I had no trouble interpreting.

"You'll be wanting the dentist next door," I said briskly. "Look for the sign that says 'Dentist,' not 'Temple of Spiritualism.'"

It never ceased to amaze me how often people made this mistake—and this in spite of the fact that the dentist's sign was embellished with an enormous set of teeth. I had threatened before to electrify those teeth, making them champ at passers-by. As I shut the door, I reflected it might be as well to make the sign more conspicuous, too. The new Edison bulbs sounded ideal for the purpose. Of course one would need something like a dynamo to run them—batteries would hardly answer the purpose—but I had been considering investing in a dynamo anyway. It would save a lot of trouble mucking about with glass jars and ammonium chloride.

Shelving this idea for later consideration, I went back to the Sitting Room to find Inspector Harper asleep on the sofa, his unshaven cheek pillowed on his folded arm.

I didn't have the heart to wake him, Dear Reader. So I fetched my account books, sat down beside him, and figured accounts while he slept. The poor man would have to go back on patrol in a matter of hours, since tonight was the dark of the moon. It wasn't the way I would have chosen to employ those hours, but at least he wasn't with Mrs. McIntyre.

Chapter 16

It was a relief to wake up the next morning and not hear the newsboys in the street crying, "Another horrid murder!"

That didn't mean there hadn't *been* another horrid murder, of course. The last victim, Miss Gowd, hadn't been discovered until some days after her death. I found myself hoping that if the murderer had struck last night, he had concealed the body well enough so it wouldn't be found till after the premier of *Night and Day*.

I knew this to be a selfish attitude, Dear Reader. Not only did I know it, I even felt guilty about it. You can't associate with idealistic people like Jenny and Inspector Harper without being infected with their ideals to some extent. But the pragmatic part of my mind sensibly noted that if the victim was already dead, it couldn't matter to *her* when her body was found.

In the same pragmatic spirit, I went through the newspapers at breakfast, skipping over the latest theories about the New Moon Murderer to see what was written about my opera. Advertisements had appeared weeks ago promising "a thrilling NEW spectacle, unequalled on the British stage." Now, as opening night approached, Mr. Hinney had pulled out all the stops and was giving full play to the Spiritualistic aspect of the work. By and large, the press had responded with enthusiasm.

"The First Opera Ever Written through Spirit Control," trumpeted one article. Another was portentously headed, "Dead Composer Speaks from Beyond the Grave to Finish Last Work."

I thought that would annoy Mr. Witters. Technically *he* was the composer, not Signor Russo. Several newspapers had made this mistake, but most did at least mention Mr. Witters's having a hand in the business.

"Mr. Percival Witters, the celebrated English composer, has joined forces with Spiritualist Madame Seraphina Fox to create this unique work, which brings to completion the final, unfinished libretto of Roberto Russo," read one of the more accurate articles. "Mr. Russo's untimely death has been much lamented among opera-goers around the globe. A true cosmopolitan, writing in the Italian, French, and English languages, his works include *Charlemagne*; *She Walks in Beauty*; *J'y suis, j'y reste*; and *Basta e Basta*, the last of which introduced the prodigious talents of soprano Paola Mazzara. Miss Mazzara will be performing the leading rôle in *Night and Day*, Mr. Russo's posthumous work, adding further lustre to a production that already promises to be of outstanding interest to the opera world."

I was pleased to see that Signora Mazzara received favourable mention in this and other articles. No one was tactless enough to mention that last *Lucia* at La Scala. Some of the papers were a bit snide about *my* role, however. "A Truly 'Spirited' Opera? Or a Fraud on the Opera-Going Public?" inquired the *Banner* disagreeably. I wasn't pleased about that, naturally, but comforted myself with the reflection that no right-thinking person would credit anything the *Banner* printed anyway.

I was just folding the papers away when Susan appeared, wearing an expression that portended trouble. "Miss Toth is here," she said. "Do you want to see her?"

My hand went automatically to my revolver. I was still lugging it around, Dear Reader, though feeling it was probably unnecessary at this point. Whenever I tried to convince myself it was safe to leave it off, however, I seemed to feel that knife at my throat again. Something about that experience had left me feeling very fragile and vulnerable. The revolver seemed to assuage these feelings to some extent. At any rate, it did no harm, apart from the nuisance of its weight and bulk beneath my skirts. And now that I was about to be confronted once again with Miss Toth, my would-be murderer, I felt downright glad I still had it with me.

"Show her in," I told Susan. "But stay within earshot. You might call Jenny to stand guard, too, if she's back from the baker's."

I stood, hand on hidden revolver, watching as Miss Toth came into the room. She was wearing the same shapeless greeny-yellow dress she had worn last time and a bonnet of surpassing ugliness. For a moment she paused, regarding me timidly. Then she flung herself at my feet with sudden abandon.

"Madame Fox," she said with a sob, "you must help us. You *must*."

I could not help recoiling, Dear Reader. Just having her so close to me was unwelcome. Having her weeping over my boots was not only unwelcome but embarrassing. "Help you?" I repeated, trying to shuffle my feet out of her grasp. "What am I to help you do?"

"Save Absalom," she said, with another heart-rending sob. "The police think he's a murderer, but he's not! I know he's not. You must help us."

In as heartening a manner as possible, I explained that her brother had nothing to fear if he was innocent. "The British Justice system is outstanding for seeing that all accused persons get fair play," I assured her.

Miss Toth gave a gulp—or it might have been a snort, Dear Reader. "But we're not British," she said. "We're American—foreigners. The police here don't like us. I can tell they don't. They want Absalom to be guilty."

I thought very likely they did, Dear Reader. Possibly it had something to do with Mr. Toth's being American, though it probably owed more to his being such a strange, unlikeable creature. Indeed, there was something unlikeable about all the Toths.

"I don't know what you expect me to do," I told Miss Toth. "If you feel your brother has been unjustly detained by the police, you would do better to engage a good solicitor[15] to defend him."

"Mother's already done that," said Miss Toth with another shuddering sob. "She engaged a solicitor as soon as he was arrested. Both of us are doing all we can. But then I thought of you and realized you might be able to do something more. The Spirits," she explained, looking up at me with tear-drenched eyes.

---

[15] The British legal system differs materially from the American, and in nothing so much as the titles of its practitioners. What is called a lawyer in the States might in Britain be either a barrister or solicitor. The latter term is particularly confusing to Americans, who associate it rather with those who sell Thin Mints and vacuum cleaners door-to-door.—*Ed.*

"They knew it was I who came here planning to kill you. Don't you think they could tell who really killed those women?"

I was filled with quite unjustifiable irritation, Dear Reader. After all, I had set myself up as an all-seeing Oracle. She was only taking me at my word.

I put on a distant, inscrutable manner. "All things are known on the Other Side," I said. "But Spiritual communications can be rather cryptic."

"Mr. Thoreau might help, if you ask him," offered Miss Toth. "You remember those beautiful words he spoke to us a few weeks ago." In a reverent voice, she quoted, "'The truth shall prevail and falsehood discover itself, as long as the wind blows on the hills.'"

I did not enjoy having my own Spiritual communications thrown back in my face. "Yes," I said, after a pause. "There's that, of course."

"I feel certain you can find out the truth," she went on eagerly. "I don't know why I didn't think of it sooner. Or why Mother didn't think of it. But she is quite upset about this business, of course—and also a trifle upset with you, Madame Fox. Just as I was." She met my eyes fleetingly, then looked away, blushing. "She has only just found out it was you who told the police about Absalom and that woman."

I felt a faint premonitory chill. Of the two female Toths, I had no doubt the elder was the more formidable when roused. Heaven knew her daughter had been formidable enough. I made a mental note to deny myself should Mrs. Toth appear on my doorstep, wanting to talk to me.

"I am very sorry that you and your mother have been put to so much trouble," I said aloud. "It was through no wish of mine, believe me."

Miss Toth nodded. "I do understand that now, Madame Fox. I'm sure Mother will understand it, too, once she has time to consider." She gave me a smile that was childlike in its perfect assurance. "And even if she doesn't, she's certain to forgive you once you find out from the Spirits who the real murderer is."

***

Susan's expression spoke volumes as she showed Miss Toth to the door. After shutting it behind her, she turned to look at me. "I know," I said, holding up a hand to prevent the jeremiad I could see was coming. "I'm in a bit of a pickle. Make a note that after this, I am not at home to *any* of the Toths." Returning to the Sitting Room, I dropped down onto the sofa. Susan followed me into the room and stood there with elbows akimbo, looking down at me.

"Aren't you going to tell the Inspector?" she asked.

"Tell him what?" I demanded. "It's not as though Miss Toth gave us any new information. Except that Mrs. Toth is angry with me, which was only to be expected."

Susan, with stubborn insistence, said the Inspector ought to know. "It might help him solve the case. I'm not convinced myself she's out of it. She did try to kill you, after all."

I gave way after a short struggle, Dear Reader. In fact, I wasn't sorry to have an excuse to summon the Inspector, though

I felt sure it would be the briefest of interviews. We were only a night off the dark of the moon, and doubtless the police would be out in force tonight, too, just to be on the safe side.

It was indeed a brief interview, but not without interest. Inspector Harper was once again clad in sailor's garb, for which he once again apologized. I said it would only make the glory of him in full evening dress shine all the brighter the following night, at which he smiled.

"It does look as though I'll be able to attend your opera," he said. "No murder last night—not even the usual kind of murder that might happen on any night. In fact, crime in general's been down these last few days. Barring any incident tonight, we ought to be all set."

"I suppose Inspector Freemantle now feels vindicated in his theory," I said.

Inspector Harper nodded, looking resigned. "He's not crowing about it yet, which is sensible," he said. "After all, we didn't find Miss Gowd's body until some days after the dark of the moon. But yes, if nothing more develops over the next few days, it would seem to show Ned is right and Toth is the responsible party." He looked at me curiously. "You said you had something new that bore on the case?"

"Not really," I said. "I had a visit from Miss Toth earlier today, and Susan thought you ought to know about it. I went ahead and put it in transcript form, but I warn you in advance there's not much in it."

He read through the transcript carefully, and I watched him as he read, noting how pronounced the lines on his face appeared—owing to fatigue, no doubt. I could have sworn his cheeks were a shade hollower, too. Likely Mrs. McIntyre had been stinting him again. I was just about to ring the bell for refreshments when he looked up, and the expression on his face made me forget everything else.

"You mustn't see these people anymore," he said. "Not any of them, Seraphina. Please don't risk it. Tell your servants to deny you if they call again."

In some surprise, I told him I had already given such an order. "But what is it, Tom? Have you caught something in the transcript I missed?"

"It's just an idea," he said. "There might be nothing in it. Or perhaps it's just that I sustained a very unpleasant interview with Mrs. Toth yesterday that may have affected my judgment."

He was silent a moment, contemplating me. "Tell me," he said at last, "when we were discussing the idea of Miss Toth's guilt a while back, you mentioned that she was accustomed to wearing pantaloons. Men's clothing, that is, according to most people's way of thinking."

"Yes," I agreed. "The Toths lived for a time in a commune in the States where all the women wore pantaloons."

"Then wouldn't that mean that Mrs. Toth is equally accustomed to wearing them?"

For a moment I gaped at him. "You think *she* might be the second man?"

"It's at least a possibility," he said. "She's about her son's height and as thin as he is—in fact, all three of them are walking skeletons. In men's clothes, from a distance, she would probably resemble him pretty closely. Moreover, she's got a motive that's at least as good as his."

I was having trouble wrapping my mind around this idea. "You think *Mrs. Toth* might be the New Moon Murderer? Oh, but it's ludicrous."

"Is it? Think about it. She would have a grudge against prostitutes. According to her way of thinking, they are responsible for her son's . . . weakness. And there's nothing whatever about these crimes that would preclude a woman's having committed them. Remember the murderer had no sexual connection with the victims. He—or she—purposely arranged for them to face away from him in a vulnerable position. Armed with a sharp knife—and the weapon in all these crimes was a very sharp knife—a woman could have cut their throats quite as easily as a man."

On considering the idea, I found it held a certain credibility. "Of all the family, Mrs. Toth does strike me as the most ruthless," I agreed. "The fact that she's an idealist doesn't conflict with that at all. On the contrary: she's the kind of idealist whose idealism is really a mask for intolerance. If you're one-hundred-per-cent assured you're right, you aren't about to accept dissenting opinions."

"Yes," he agreed. "I certainly felt that way after talking to her. I could see her dealing very ruthlessly with anyone whom she felt had injured or threatened her."

"But is there evidence to show she actually is the New Moon Murderer?"

He made a helpless gesture. "How could there be? We've never investigated her—never even had cause to investigate her. The idea only came to me after reading your transcript."

"The part about her being angry with me?" I said. "That did give me a bit of a turn when her daughter told me about it. But of course, it's natural that she should be angry."

"Yes," he said. "But it's not natural that her adult children should go in such fear of her. And there's another thing that struck me as unnatural, even before this latest business came up. Don't you think it's a trifle remarkable that both the younger Toths seem able to leave the house at night whenever they please? If their mother rules over them with an iron hand during the day, you'd think she'd do it at night, too."

"But if she were leaving the house herself at night, that would explain it," I said, catching the idea. "Yes, it's possible, I suppose. Are you going to investigate her?"

He shook his head slowly. "As matters now stand, we have a much more credible suspect in her son. I'd be laughed out of Scotland Yard for suggesting such a theory at this point." He thought a moment, running a hand absently through his hair. "If we're forced to release Mr. Toth later on, I might be able to do it. The Chief would be desperate enough then to embrace almost any theory. For the last few months the Home Secretary's demanded a personal report every day, to explain why we haven't yet found who's responsible for these crimes." He half-smiled, shaking his head again. "Absalom Toth is giving him a respite at present. But if that proves only temporary, the Chief will need someone to propose as a replacement."

I remarked that it was no wonder Mrs. Toth was upset, if indeed she was the murderer. "She has gone unsuspected all these months, and now it appears her son might pay the penalty for her crimes. That would be an irony, wouldn't it?"

"Yes," he said. "And if it's so, she's a dangerous woman. You must be on your guard."

I said I was a dangerous woman, too, surreptitiously touching my revolver. The Inspector merely laughed, a trifle ruefully. "I've reason to know it," he said. "But *she* may not." The idea seemed to worry him; before he left, he urged me again to be on my guard.

"I shall be," I said. "And just to be on the safe side, I intend to take your advice and provide myself with police protection—for tomorrow night, at least."

Laughter sprang up in his eyes. "A fine idea," he agreed.

Together we arranged the details of when we would meet and how he would come to fetch me. As he took leave of me at the door, I told him to be on his guard, too. "After all, it's you who go abroad at night looking for murderers."

"Yes, but that's my job," he said, adding with emphasis, "*not* yours."

I pointed out that I had been of use to him once or twice in this regard. He acknowledged it very handsomely. "But we're dealing with a more than usually dangerous criminal in this case," he said. "Someone who's killed half-a-dozen times and wouldn't hesitate to kill again. If you'd stick to Spiritualism from here on out, I would be a lot happier. Which reminds me." He looked at me, his head tilted to one side. "No new word from the Spirits, I suppose?"

It struck me as something more than coincidence, Dear Reader. Both he and Miss Toth had mentioned my consulting the Spirits. Now that I considered it, I realized that I might do so—in the form of Felicity, at least. Even if she had nothing new in the way of information, she might have a practical idea about how to proceed. "I consulted them a few weeks ago, but they had nothing of moment to add then," I said. "Perhaps it's time to consult them again."

Chapter 17

I discussed the matter with Jenny and Susan at our nightly conference. They were in favour of consulting Felicity, too, albeit for slightly different reasons.

"If Mrs. Toth is a danger, you ought to take steps right away to guard against her," said Susan bluntly. "Don't wait till she comes around here with a knife like her daughter. I can see how the Inspector's hands are tied, but yours aren't."

"Yes," agreed Jenny. "Maybe Sam and I ought to start sleeping in the house again."

I told her I thought that wasn't necessary. "Miss Toth caught us off guard last time, but that won't happen again. I'll talk to Felicity, however, and see if she can help. Perhaps some of her people can keep an eye on Mrs. Toth."

"*And* her daughter," said Susan. "Say what you will, I'm still not convinced she didn't have something to do with these murders. Maybe she and her brother are both in it. Maybe they took turns killing those women—first one and then the other. I wonder if the Inspector's thought of *that*?"

"Poor man," I said. "If he hasn't, I won't plague him with the idea just now. Not unless we can get some proof that it's more than an idea. I'd like to be able to enjoy our outing tomorrow night without his work interfering."

"Yes, your opera," said Jenny. "Quite the excitement, isn't it, now it's actually coming off? I'm sure we're all proud as proud can be of you, ma'am."

Susan did not exactly endorse these sentiments but observed that I seemed to have scraped through all right, which was more than she had expected.

"I wish you two were coming with me tomorrow night," I said. "And Sam, too. There's not a reason in the world you couldn't all sit in the box with the Inspector and me. It would hold six people easily."

Jenny shook her head. "It wouldn't be fitting, ma'am," she said firmly.

"I wish I may see it," said Susan, rolling her eyes. "Me, sitting in a box at the opera, pretending to be a fine lady. No, thank you: I'll go sometime by myself and sit in the stalls."

I had given up arguing with them about it, Dear Reader. Certainly it is unconventional for a lady to attend the opera with her servants, but my household is run on far more democratic lines than is usual. I have never subscribed to the British class system. Thus, it was a shock to find them quite as prejudiced in their way as their so-called betters. I can see that in the future, I must work on inculcating them with true republican ideals.

"I shall see you get tickets, at any rate," I said aloud. "I would have gotten them before now if I'd known you weren't going to sit with me. I'm afraid the opening night performance is already sold out."

Jenny said cheerfully that she and Sam would go to the music hall tomorrow night and see the opera some other time. I had a shrewd notion the music hall was more to their taste anyway, Dear Reader. I do not mean this as any kind of a slur, for in fact I prefer the music hall myself, in the general way.

Susan cleared her throat. "As to that," she said. "I'd take it as a great favour if I might take tomorrow night off, and all day Sunday as well."

"Yes, of course," I said without hesitation. I make a point of humouring Susan's requests whenever possible, having a persistent fear that she will one day leave me for greener pastures. That would be devastating, for I could not hope to find another assistant who could match her in intellect, initiative, or discretion.

Looking at her closely now, I detected something amiss—something that struck me as worrisome. "I hope nothing is wrong?" I asked. "Do you need more than the one day? If so, you've only got to say."

She said the one day would be quite sufficient, with a finality that discouraged further inquiry. I made a mental note to keep an eye on her and her affairs just the same. If she had some personal trouble, I wanted early warning so I might help avert it, if possible.

This gave me something new to worry about, which I didn't feel I needed just then. I already had worries in plenty—mostly connected with *Night and Day*. In addition to worrying whether Mr. Cardle's heart would keep him from singing tomorrow evening, and whether the "Moonlight" ballet would have to be performed without a backdrop, and whether the signora's voice would fail her at the critical moment, I had also to worry whether something might happen overnight that would keep Inspector Harper from accompanying me. I thought I really couldn't face sitting in that opera box all alone.

But the next day dawned again without the newsboys crying any new murders, and I received a note from the Inspector at breakfast time saying that all looked quite in order for the night ahead.

Although I had no sitting scheduled that evening, I did have business to transact during the day. My chief business was to visit my dressmaker, from whom I had ordered a dress for the opera premier. In the usual fashion of dressmakers, she had drawn out the business until the last possible moment. I actually had to wait while the last stitches were set. Once it was safely stowed in the brougham, I drew a sigh of relief. "To the Calico Cat, Sam, please. You may drop me there and then take these packages back to the Temple. I'll take a cab home when I'm ready to go."

***

I found Felicity in her usual place by the fire. She waved a hand as I entered—a hand holding a smoking pipe. As I came closer, I saw this was not her only masculine accessory. She was wearing men's boots, too, clearly visible beneath a skirt of pepper-and-salt tweed that barely covered her knees. For the rest, she had on striped stockings, a shabby green serge jacket, and a squashed-looking hat with a bunch of cherries on it.

"My dear Seraphina," she said. "Sit down and have a cuppa."

"My dear Felicity," I replied. "I should be delighted."

I was glad of the tea after the bustle of the dressmaker's. Felicity urged muffins and tea-cakes upon me, then settled back to survey me appraisingly. "You look like you're in a bit of a pother, dear," she said.

"I am," I admitted, and told her what had been happening.

Felicity is the best of listeners, Dear Reader. Undoubtedly this is part of her genius. It is so enjoyable to confide in her that one ends up confiding more than one intends. I was quite startled when she observed that the Inspector and I were growing thick as thieves, seemingly. I had no reply to make to that, which caused her to smile shrewdly and remark that he was a taking man by all accounts.

As I had no reply for that, either, I sought to change the subject. "It's this business of the New Moon Murderer that I really wanted to consult with you about," I said. "If it's Mrs. Toth rather than her son who killed those women, then she is still at large and possibly dangerous."

Felicity drew on her pipe, surveying me again with a thoughtful eye. "I don't quite follow you, dear," she said. "What makes you think this woman's the murderer any more than her son?"

I explained at length about the second man, and the female Toths' predilection for wearing pantaloons, and Mr. Toth's apparent alibi for the last murder.

"Aye," she said. "I've been wondering about that myself. I saw where he's been arrested, but for the life of me I don't understand why. He hadn't the least chance to murder that poor woman, any more than you or I."

"You think not?" I said dubiously.

"I know it," she returned. "I was there, you see."

For a moment I felt as though the wind had been knocked out of me. Felicity kindly advised me to drink some tea, and pushed the sugar bowl toward me. "I can see that shocks you, dear," she said. "But there's no mystery about it. You'd told me about the young man and how he might be the murderer. That being the case, I reckoned it'd be as well to keep an eye on him."

"Yes," I said. "Of course. I remember now." I remembered also that I had been afraid Felicity might wreak her own private vengeance on Absalom Toth without benefit of judge, jury, or hangman.

She clearly remembered it, too, for she grinned. "You were set against me taking measures of my own," she said, "but I didn't think it'd do any harm to keep the young man under my eye. Just on the chance I might do some good, you understand."

I thought I understood, all right. If Felicity had witnessed Absalom Toth committing murder, she would have considered it an excuse to break her promise—a promise she had not wanted to give in the first place. I was too excited to dwell long on this point, however.

"If you were following Mr. Toth that night," I said, "then you must have seen the second man. He's the one we think might truly be the murderer. Or *she* might be, if it turns out to have been Miss Toth or Mrs. Toth dressed in men's clothes."

Felicity shook her head. "You keep talking about this second man," she said, "but I'm blessed if I know what you mean."

I set myself to explain it all over again. "On the night of Lizzie Gowd's murder, Absalom Toth was being trailed by two policemen." I paused here, looking at her to be sure she followed me thus far.

"Aye, *that* I know," she said at once. "Great flat-footed creatures they were, too. Anybody might have guessed they was police. I wonder Toth himself didn't guess it."

"He did notice one of them, but thought nothing of it," I said. "He had an assignation with a woman that night. Not Miss Gowd, but another—er—woman of pleasure. That's where he was going."

"To Elsie Ramsbottom," said Felicity, nodding. "At Annie Sackett's house. I followed him there—saw him go in—had a drink with Annie while they were upstairs and found out all about it."

"Then you *must* have seen the second man. The police were following Mr. Toth that night, just as you were. But at some point, he was joined by another man who looked very much like him. In fact, he looked so much like him that the police couldn't tell which was which. Eventually Mr. Toth and the other man—the second man—parted and went their separate ways. The police split up to follow them both, but by bad luck the less competent of the two was deputed to follow Toth and lost him right away."

I looked at Felicity to see if she were still following me. She nodded, her expression intent. "The other policeman, who's a detective inspector, followed the second man for a while. But he soon realized his man wasn't Mr. Toth and turned back. Which is too bad, because there's a distinct possibility now that the second man might have been the murderer, on his way to murder Miss Gowd."

Felicity shook her head. "I never saw any second man," she said, "barring the two policemen you was talking about. Of course there was a few drayman and carters and so forth on the streets. Could it be one of them you mean?"

"No," I said, "though of course there *were* other men about. And a few women, too. Mr. Toth admits as much, though he disclaims any knowledge of the man we're interested in. The only person he admits to talking to during his walk was a woman."

"That was me," said Felicity proudly.

"Was it indeed?" I exclaimed. "How very curious! But the second man couldn't have been a drayman or carter or any other working man. For the police said he was dressed just like Mr. Toth and walking right beside him."

"Nobody did that," said Felicity flatly. "Mr. Toth was all by himself, all the way to Sackett's."

Again, I was staggered. "Are you sure?" I asked. She gave me a look that made me apologize immediately. "I do beg your pardon, Felicity! But this is so unexpected. I can't think how such a mistake can have been made."

She nodded. "Aye, it's a queer mistake, all right." She sat silent for a moment, apparently reliving the events of that night in her head. "I remember," she said presently. "I remember the two policemen splitting up. I remember one of them followed on for a while, after Toth. Then he turned back sudden-like, and I didn't see any more of either of them."

"That must have been P.C. Cobden," I said. "But how strange. How very strange that you never saw another man with Mr. Toth. I don't know what to make of it."

Felicity threw me a shrewd look. "Easy enough to explain," she said. "Police is human just like the rest of us. It was a dirty night, and one or both of 'em likely just wanted an excuse to stop and warm himself at a public house over a pint or two."

I nodded, a trifle dubiously. Certainly the police like to be out of the cold and wet as much as any of us, Dear Reader. They likewise appreciate a drop of refreshment from time to time, even being known to take it during hours of duty despite regulations to the contrary. But I could not believe that Inspector Freemantle would have done it on that night—the night when all London was on alert for another murder.

Even if he had, the report he had submitted seemed deliberately misleading, not merely an excuse for negligence. His fellow officers had put in countless hours of investigation, based on the idea that there had been a second man that evening with Absalom Toth. I was more inclined to suspect he had submitted a false report to throw his colleagues off the scent, while he and P.C. Cobden pursued some private clue they hoped would lead them to the New Moon Murderer.

Once I had thought of it, I felt satisfied this was the true explanation. It seemed exactly like something Inspector Freemantle would do. As I sat musing on the subject, I was startled by Felicity's next words.

"I've another bit of news for you," she said, "which you might pass on to that Inspector of yours. You was telling me how the two of you had been investigating Peg Henley's accommodation house, and how you'd found a peephole in the room where Mattie Bird was killed?"

"Yes," I said, "but as a clue, it turned out to be a dead end. Mrs. Henley claimed to know nothing about it."

Felicity snorted. "'Course she did. But she knows, all right. I spent some time talking to her servants, and they tell me she uses that peephole all the time, *and* others like it. It's a regular sideline of hers. She sees who goes into the rooms and keeps notes on dates and times and so forth, just in case it's somebody she might be able to put the black on later."

"*Blackmail*," I breathed. "That did occur to us, early on. It would be one of the obvious uses for a spyhole in that sort of room. But do you think Mrs. Henley saw something the night Miss Bird was killed?"

"Odds are she at least saw who was there," said Felicity. "It wouldn't be like her to neglect such a chance, from everything I hear."

At first I was very excited by this news, Dear Reader. When I thought it over, however, I realized it all still hinged on Mrs. Henley telling the truth to the police. So far she had refused to do so. And she had reason, if she was running a sideline in blackmail as well as condoning immoral activity on her premises. But it seemed at least possible that with Felicity's information, the police might be able to find new evidence against the murderer.

I put all this information by to tell the Inspector later, for I had no time to think any more about it just then. Bidding Felicity farewell, I went home to bathe, dress, and adorn myself for *Night and Day*.

Chapter 18

In *Walden*, his best-known work, Henry David Thoreau advises his readers to beware of enterprises requiring new clothes.

I consider it some of his less practical advice, Dear Reader. Doubtless many a noble heart beats beneath a shabby coat; we all will admit the point. But Human Nature being what it is, the owner of both heart and coat will find his fellow men and women judge him more by the latter rather than the former, as being the more visible of the two.

Indeed, few of us are philosophers enough to be oblivious even to our own raiment. It is a comfort to be well-dressed—a comfort and (with apologies to Mr. Thoreau) oftentimes a pleasure. And when one is sitting in an opera box, the focus of hundreds of eyes and opera glasses, it is pleasure of a very exalted sort to know they have something worth looking at, even when it is only one's outer shell (so to speak).

Mr. Hinney had come through handsomely in the way of seating. My box was on the Grand Tier, just beside the one traditionally reserved for Royalty. To appear to advantage in it, I had shed my customary black and blossomed forth in a dress of purple brocade threaded and laced with gold. This barbarically splendid garment had been modeled on the robes worn by an ancient priestess of Astarte—or rather what an ancient priestess of Astarte might wear if interpreted by a nineteenth-century dressmaker. That is to say, it had a bustle behind and a corset beneath, and it did not leave my bosom *entirely* bare, though it came pretty close. It was amusing to see Inspector Harper trying not to notice.

In addition to this startling garment, I wore a tiara set with amethysts in the shape of a star, along with a matching necklace. They were, admittedly, not *real* amethysts, and the gold of both tiara and necklace was only skin-deep. But it should be obvious by now, Dear Reader, that I am comfortable with a degree of fraudulence. A certain amount of my hair was fraudulent as well, and I had touched up my eyes and complexion to appear at my best.

On beholding me for the first time in this attire, Inspector Harper's mouth had fallen open. When he had finally been able to speak, he had spluttered out words to the effect that he would be the envy of every other man there, to appear in company with such a beautiful woman.

I treasured the compliment even while I discounted it, Dear Reader. Illusion is my business, and I am very good at it, but whomever else we deceive, we shouldn't deceive ourselves. Still, I reckoned with some complacency that from a distance I wasn't likely to be outshone by anyone that night, at least until Signora Mazzara stepped onto the stage.

The Inspector, for his part, looked entirely handsome and distinguished. I told him so, Dear Reader, and without any spluttering, either. The austerity of formal dress suited him far better than most men. Whatever Mr. Thoreau might say, the consciousness of being well-dressed made a difference to us both—in the way we moved and spoke, and in the way we looked at each other. At the moment, we were being very courtly and formal, but there was a tension underlying the formality that made the atmosphere between us slightly electric. I reckoned I had a decent chance of seducing him before the night was over.

As the members of the orchestra were tuning their instruments, a movement in the next box caught my eye. "Look," I said, nudging the Inspector to draw his attention to it. "There's Mr. Witters, the composer."

Mr. Witters was by himself. His hair was standing on end as usual, and though he wore formal attire like the Inspector, his was slightly rumpled. He settled into his seat with the dour expression of a man prepared for the worst.

"Poor fellow," whispered Inspector Harper in my ear. "He looks dyspeptic."

"That's just his usual expression," I whispered back. "And it's likely to get worse before it gets better—judging by his reaction to the last rehearsal, anyway."

A moment later, the orchestra launched into the overture. I drew a deep breath and tried to relax—a manoeuvre not assisted by my tight-laced corset.

The curtain lifted to reveal a lush tropical landscape bathed in the rays of a setting sun. The audience was given a moment to appreciate it, and then the airship came sailing in from stage left. It was painted gold, and the propellers were slowly turning as it settled upon the stage. There were oohs and ahs, and a spontaneous burst of applause. I beamed. "That was *my* idea," I told the Inspector, conveniently forgetting my debt to Monsieur Verne.

Lucien and Apollo dismounted from their airship, and were joined a moment later by the men of the chorus. They all wore white uniforms heavily embellished with gold braid. Those who were not naturally blond had been given blond wigs. They looked Men of Light indeed: quite a dazzling spectacle. Lucien, as their leader, wore a uniform even more splendid than the others, though the rotundity of Mr. Cardle's figure did not necessarily set it off to fullest advantage. Still, he was an impressive figure and seemed to be in good voice, as I observed to the Inspector in an undertone.

"He claims to have suffered a heart attack last week," I whispered, "but Mr. Hinney thought it was just a bilious fit."

The Inspector said appearances would support Mr. Hinney's theory. "He may be a Man of Light, but he looks like a heavy feeder."

The chorus's song was well-received. So was the duet between Lucien and Apollo. Glancing at Mr. Witters, I thought he looked a degree less disapproving. The curtain came down; the audience applauded; and when the curtain rose again, it was to reveal a twilight landscape of dark trees and strange, pale flowers. A rocky grotto loomed at stage right. Lucien appeared and declared himself lost and frightened by the coming darkness.

"I've had the same feeling," whispered the Inspector in my ear, "when I was patrolling the East End docks in the fog."

I tried to frown at him, failed, and ended up giggling like a schoolgirl. A couple of people turned to look at me disapprovingly. I stared back at them until they looked away.

Under cover of the box railing, the Inspector's hand stole out to mine. I seized hold of it, glad of the reassurance. "Now for the signora," I whispered.

Her entrance evoked a burst of applause. She was wearing flowing dark robes in this early scene, not unlike those worn by Miss Dart, but more elaborate. On her veiled head was a coronet topped with a sparkling crescent moon. Her staff was likewise topped with a crescent moon.

She acknowledged the applause with a regal bow and smile, then began her song about the flowers. To the Inspector, in an undertone, I pointed out her folly in laying aside her staff without looking to see if there were dangerous characters about.

"An elementary mistake," he agreed. "One should always keep one's weapon close at hand. You either learn it early in the force, or you don't have a chance to learn it at all!"

I nodded, letting the fingers of my other hand stray to the outline of the revolver beneath my skirt. Even in this setting, I had not felt comfortable leaving it off.

The confrontation between Melanie and Lucien followed, during which the stage lights gradually faded and mist began to swirl. A thunderous burst from the orchestra heralded the arrival of the Goblin King. As his shadowy figure took form in the entrance of the grotto, the audience fell silent. Looking around, I saw nothing but rapt faces and staring eyes.

When finally he stood revealed, a huge figure in grey rags, there was wild applause. His basso aria was received with wild applause, too. In fact, I thought he was applauded more enthusiastically than the signora had been in *her* opening song.

There was something in her rigid figure and glittering eye that suggested she had noticed this, too. But of course she was confronting both her hereditary enemy and the Goblin King, which would suffice to explain it. In any case, the fight between Lucien and the King enabled her to retrieve her staff, and she drove the Goblin King back underground, accompanied by a shower of sparks that drew enthusiastic applause. Looking somewhat appeased, she launched into her duet with Lucien, "Is This My Enemy?"

"Very nice," said the Inspector, smiling at me. "Very allegorical."

"I don't know what you mean," I said, squeezing his hand.

This duet was roundly applauded, and that further appeased the signora. But it was her duet with the contralto Susan/Egeria that roused the most enthusiasm. "*Encore*," screamed a gentleman in the pit, jumping up and down like a jack-in-the-box. The cry of "*encore*" was taken up by the audience at large, and soon the theatre resounded with it.

The signora glanced at Miss Dart, shrugged, and nodded to the orchestra leader. In his box across the way, Mr. Witters folded his arms across his chest and scowled. Despite the compliment to his score, he obviously disapproved of suspending the action in this artificial way.

While the soprano and contralto voices mingled harmoniously once more, I explained to the Inspector about the foolish operatic convention that associated greater age and lesser rôles with the contralto voice. He agreed it was very vexing. "Of course I could hardly have given Miss Dart the leading rôle," I said, "seeing that the signora was commissioning the opera for herself. But if I ever wrote another opera, I would make sure we contraltos received our innings."

Apollo's aria, "Deeds of Darkness," followed, and that was encored, too. This finished the first act. I expressed my relief to the Inspector that it had gone so well.

"Do you care to go to the saloon and get an ice?" he asked.

"Between you and me, I would rather have something stronger," I said. "I won't be able to relax until the signora's aria in the next act comes off. If it does," I added, with a touch of foreboding.

We got a lot of stares in the lobby. I smiled graciously and nodded to anyone who caught my eye. The Inspector and I had a drink together in the saloon, and then I excused myself and went to the ladies' retiring room. The weight of the tiara and false hair combined were beginning to give me a headache. I adjusted them so as to relieve the pressure, then joined the Inspector outside. He was leaning against the wall, looking around at the other opera-goers. "I don't see any sign of security," he said disapprovingly. "You'd think they'd be worried about theft. There must be a king's ransom in jewels here tonight."

I told him he could take it up with Mr. Hinney after the performance, and together we returned to our box.

The second act began with the procession of the Women of Darkness. It was a beautiful scene with coloured mists drifting across the darkened stage, a huge glowing full moon rising behind, and the women's voices swelling as they followed their leader onstage with lighted lanterns in hand. Once formed in a circle around their Sacred Grove, the signora made an imperious gesture with her staff, and the dancers came on to perform the "Moonlight" ballet.

"Very pretty indeed," said the Inspector, applauding with the rest of the audience.

"I didn't have much to do with this part," I told him honestly. "But I'm glad you like it."

We were nearing the critical moment now. I could hardly appreciate Lucien's next aria, expressing first disbelief of the truth Melanie told him and then a growing conviction. It was well-received, but hardly had the applause subsided when the orchestra struck up the opening notes of "Do You Not Dream?" I squeezed the Inspector's hand tighter.

"If she doesn't manage that high A," I whispered, "it's likely to get ugly very quickly. By all accounts she was practically mobbed at La Scala. Have your handcuffs at the ready, Tom, and be prepared to read the riot act."

He merely smiled and said he doubted that would be necessary with an English audience. Despite his reassurance, I listened with mounting anxiety as the signora's voice rose higher and higher. And then—there it was. Full and strong it came forth, at that almost inhuman pitch.

The audience sat up as though electrified—and "electrified" was absolutely the proper word. Remembering again the way the Spiritograph had chimed when she had sung in the Spirit Parlour, I wondered if there might be an electrical quality to such sounds. The evidence would seem to indicate it, Dear Reader.

In any case, there was triumph in every line of the signora's figure as she finished the last measures of her aria. A moment's pause, and then the applause rolled forth, wave after wave of it. "*Brava, brava*," screamed the excitable gentleman in the pit, jumping up and down once again. *"Encore, encore."*

I wouldn't have thought she would attempt it, Dear Reader, but she did. Not only did she sing it again, she sang it with extra trills and flourishes that hadn't been there the first time.

Mr. Witters, in the neighbouring box, buried his face in his hands.

I thought I could understand why, looking at it from his point of view. She didn't make even a pretence of singing it in the guise of Melanie. She sang it directly to the audience as Signora Paola Mazzola, *prima donna*—and they loved it. I felt as pleased and proud as though I had done it all myself. In fact, such was my delight that somehow or other I found myself embracing the Inspector, right there in full view of the audience. I drew back hastily, apologizing, but he didn't seem to mind. In any case, no one was paying any attention to *us*.

The rest of the opera was distinctly anti-climactic, Dear Reader, though I hasten to say it went very well. The Goblins were vanquished through the joint efforts of Men and Women; Apollo died in an access of repentance; and Melanie and Lucien sailed away in their airship, bringing the curtain down. It came up again to reveal the cast assembled onstage to receive their due of applause. Again the curtain came down; and then went up again, over and over while the audience stamped and shouted and applauded.

They were not done applauding when a knock came on the door of our box. "Mr. Hinney's compliments," said a boy, poking his head through the door. "He'd be pleased if you'd come around backstage. They're having a bit of a party to celebrate."

We followed the boy backstage, threading our way through crowds of excited opera-goers, until we reached the room where the performers were gathered. Mr. Hinney was there, too, grinning widely, a cigar clenched in his teeth and his arm thrown around the shoulders of the Goblin King. He hailed me and the Inspector with pleasure.

"Looks like a hit," he said, offering a hand to the Inspector and then a cigar. "Paola put it across in fine shape, didn't she? Lord, but I was shaking in my shoes when she launched into that encore!"

"I don't think Mr. Witters approved," I said, glancing over to where the composer stood, arms folded across his chest once more and his expression glowering.

Mr. Hinney laughed. "Percy has his concerns and I have mine," he said. "We're sold out through the end of the month already. I don't see any reason why we shouldn't run till Christmas if the reviews are half as good as I think they'll be."

We chatted a little more, and then I went to offer my congratulations to the singers. I went out of my way to compliment Miss Dart, feeling that we contraltos ought to support each other. "You were wonderful tonight," I told her. "I never heard you in better voice."

"Thank you," she said, but from the prim set of her mouth and the disapproving way her eyes lingered on my décolletage, it was easy to see my compliments were not much appreciated.

The Signora, on the other hand, appreciated them almost too much. She came sweeping down upon me, ignoring the Inspector completely in her excitement. "It was a triumph, yes?"

she said, showing all her teeth in a dazzling smile. "Ah, never have I been so happy! Such brilliance, such beauty."

I wasn't sure whether she was talking about herself in particular or the opera in general, but I agreed it had all been very brilliant and beautiful. Instantly her face assumed a wistful expression.

"But I ask myself," she said, laying a hand on her décolletage (which I freely admit eclipsed my own, Dear Reader), "I ask myself if my poor Roberto can know of my triumph. Can he can see and hear, where he is? Can he know the happiness I feel?"

I assured her that he could. "Cannot you feel him?" I asked, waving my hand dramatically to indicate the presence of a hovering Spirit. "He is watching and listening even as we speak. And he is rejoicing in your triumph. He says no angel in heaven ever sang as sweetly as you did tonight."

Her eyes blazed up at once. "Yes," she breathed, "yes, of course." And then she threw her arms around me and kissed me.

It was not a sisterly kiss, Dear Reader. When finally she released me, I was a trifle out of breath and my tiara had slipped to one side. She regarded me with a beatific smile. "For Roberto," she explained.

There was dead silence in the room. Looking around, I saw everyone was staring at us. "You English," I said, reaching up to adjust my tiara. "You English are so cold."

The Signora flitted off to greet another acquaintance, and after a while conversation started up again. Eventually, I risked a look at the Inspector. He was regarding me with fixed intensity.

Several times I thought he was going to speak, but then he appeared to think better of it.

Finally, bending down to speak directly into my ear, he said, "I don't know quite what to think of that."

"Neither do I," I said truthfully.

He looked at me a while longer, then drew a deep breath. "Now I think *I* could do with a drink."

Champagne was flowing freely at the far end of the room. As the Inspector filled glasses for us both, I noted that Mr. Cardle and Signor Adriano were standing nearby, receiving the congratulations of their friends and admirers. Shamelessly eavesdropping on their conversations, I was amused to note the difference in tone taken by Mr. Cardle (who as Lucien had received a single curtain call) and Signor Adriano (who as Apollo had received three, not to mention an encore).

"It's a rotten piece," Mr. Cardle was saying, his mouth twisted into a disapproving grimace. "Between you and me, I'd be surprised if it runs a week. These novelties never take. Really, I ought never to have taken the part. With my heart, my doctor advises against exerting myself just now. I've a good mind to let my understudy take over and step aside altogether."

"It is a *magnificent* piece," Signor Adriano was saying, his dark eyes aglow beneath his blond wig. "I tell you, my friend: I have no doubt it will enjoy a long run and become a part of the standard repertoire."

The Inspector had overheard them, too. He caught my eye and smiled. "I almost feel I'm back at the Yard," he whispered. "Those fellows aren't any more jealous of their credit than a couple of detectives working the same case."

I opened my mouth to tell him about my idea of casting the men of Scotland Yard in an opera. Then I paused, for his mention of jealousy had awakened a memory—completely forgotten till now—of what Felicity had told me that afternoon. Perhaps it was being in the presence of Lucien and Apollo with their rivalries real and imagined, but suddenly I could feel treachery where before I had only sensed ambition.

I looked at the Inspector, and found he was gazing down at me. "What is it?" he asked. "You looked stricken all at once."

"Come with me, Tom," I said, tugging on his arm. "Someplace where we can speak in private. There's something you ought to know."

Chapter 19

We found a bench down a corridor where we could sit and talk. Occasionally someone passed—a party of lingering opera-goers, or a member of the theatre staff bent on an errand—but it was sufficiently private for our purposes.

I told the Inspector exactly what Felicity had told me. "It seems there was never a second man at all, Tom. Absalom Toth was telling the truth. For one reason or another, Inspector Freemantle and P.C. Cobden saw fit to lie about it."

It was his turn to look stricken, Dear Reader. I could see it in his eyes as the implications of my information sank in. "I can't believe it," he said, after a pause. "You think your witness is reliable?"

I told him I was willing to stake my life on it.

"Then that means—O God! At the very least, it means discredit to the force. But I can't believe it of Ned, or of Cobden either. They would have had to conspire together, and what could be their purpose?"

"I wondered that myself," I said. "Tell me, what kind of man is P.C. Cobden?"

The Inspector looked at me sharply. "You think perhaps he might have—? But no, it's not possible. At least, I shouldn't have thought it was possible." He sat staring into space, his expression growing more and more distraught. "Cobden's always struck me as a thoroughly sound fellow. Not bright, of course, but no end of courage. The other fellows tease him for being slow. It's a standing joke that if you tell him a funny story on Monday, he won't laugh till Friday." He shook his head. "I should have said he was the last man to conspire in a hoax this elaborate. More than conspire, indeed, for if Toth's not guilty . . . and it was Cobden who was following him . . . and your witness saw him turn back on purpose. . . my God, no! It's not possible."

"Could you talk to him tonight?" I asked. "Would he still be on duty?"

Again, the Inspector looked at me sharply. "Yes, he would. He's got night duty all this week. That's an idea, Seraphina. This business will have to be investigated, and the sooner the better. I'll take you home and then go on to the Yard."

"No," I said, "I shall come with you. You might need me."

It was on his lips to protest, but then he paused. "Yes," he said, after a moment. "I do need you." He looked at me soberly. "This isn't the way I would have chosen our evening to end—one of the few evenings we've had to spend together. But if you're willing to come, I'd rather have you beside me than any two men I could name."

***

I was a bit overdressed for Scotland Yard, Dear Reader, but I threw my evening cloak over my shoulders and made the best of it. Like my dress, it was flamboyant—purple velvet and cloth-of-gold. But at least it covered the parts of my anatomy which the dress left bare. I pulled the hood over my tiara-decked head, and we took a cab for the yard.

Police Constable Cobden was an enormous, ox-like man with a broad face and a pair of mild brown eyes. He greeted Inspector Harper with respect and me with obvious bewilderment, then sat looking at us both. Inspector Harper opened the interview very directly.

"I have some questions," he said, "concerning the report you submitted on the tenth of last month. That was the night you and Inspector Freemantle were following Absalom Toth: the same night we believe Lizzie Gowd was murdered."

P.C. Cobden blinked. There was no other sign that the Inspector's words had been heard or understood. "Yes, sir?" he ventured, after a moment.

"You claim to have lost Toth, somewhere in the vicinity of St. Giles's churchyard."

"Yes, sir?"

"Is this true?"

There was a pause. P.C. Cobden regarded the Inspector, his brow furrowed in perplexity. "I was following him," he said at last, in a voice that laboured to make itself understood, "following the American fellow. Inspector Freemantle and I both were. But then I lost him."

"How did you come to be following him alone?"

This appeared to be an easier question. The constable answered it quite readily and with a visible air of relief. "Inspector Freemantle said I was to follow him," he said. "So I tried."

"And whom was Inspector Freemantle following?"

There was another pause. "Some other fellow?" said P.C. Cobden, hopefully.

Inspector Harper looked at him sternly. "Come, Cobden; it's I who's asking the questions," he said. "Do you know whom Inspector Freemantle was following?"

"Some other fellow," said the constable again, but with an upward inflection that betrayed his uncertainty.

"Don't you *know*?"

P.C. Cobden looked as though he were about to burst into tears. "I'm sorry, sir," he said. "It was my mistake, losing him that night. I'm dreadful sorry about it."

"Yes, yes, so you say. We'll come back to that in a moment. Right now, I am asking about the man Inspector Freemantle was following. Did you see him? Can you describe him?"

"He looked just like the American fellow," said P.C. Cobden. "Inspector Freemantle said he'd follow him, and I should follow the other."

This had the unexpected ring of truth about it. The Inspector and I exchanged glances. "And what did the other man look like?" queried Inspector Harper.

There was a long pause. "I don't know, sir," said P.C. Cobden at last, in a defeated tone. "I lost him right away. I never got much of a look at him."

"Did you get *any* kind of look at him?" said Inspector Harper. His voice was growing more and more strained. I wondered if his thoughts were keeping pace with mine.

Again there was a pause. "No, sir," admitted the constable.

"Did you see him at all?"

"No, sir," said the constable, his voice now barely a whisper. "Inspector Freemantle said I should follow him and pointed out the way, but somehow I missed it. I looked and looked, but I never caught sight of him at all."

Inspector Harper drew a deep breath, and again his eyes met mine. "Yes," I said, answering the thought in both our minds. "It was like a joke. A joke he knew wouldn't be understood."

"My God," said the Inspector, his own voice now barely a whisper. P.C. Cobden sat looking at him with anxious, uncomprehending eyes.

"I'm very sorry, sir," he said again.

The Inspector roused himself. "It's not your fault, Cobden," he said. "But you'll need to write another report. A report stating exactly what you've just told me."

"Write a report, sir?" It was easy to see that this was hard labour as far as P.C. Cobden was concerned.

"Yes, a report," said Inspector Harper with a touch of impatience. "Right away, too—the matter is urgent." In a voice that strove to sound matter-of-fact, he asked, "Is Inspector Freemantle about?"

"No, sir; he's off duty till tomorrow."

"Very well, Cobden. I'll talk to him then . . . if not before."

***

The two of us were silent as we left Scotland Yard. The Inspector hailed a cab and put me into it, absently. "Where are we going?" I asked.

He looked at me with a blank expression. "I don't know. My God, Ned Freemantle! I don't know what I should do. If he's the one who's been. . .." He broke off, with a glance at the cab driver. "I don't know what I should do."

"If you will allow me to make a suggestion," I said, "I think it might be worth paying a call on Mrs. Henley."

He seized on this suggestion at once. "Yes, of course. The woman who runs the accommodation house where Miss Bird was murdered. If your source is right, she can describe the murderer."

"And that means she's in danger if the murderer ever suspects it," I pointed out. "Which he might, at any moment. Knowing what you know now, you might be able to convince her to talk. At any rate, I don't think you should risk waiting till tomorrow."

"Yes," he agreed. "Just let me fetch my notebook." Having provided himself with this adjunct, he gave the address to the cab driver and joined me in the cab. As we rattled down the street, he added with a touch of morbid humour, "Although it's getting late, I imagine we'll find her at home. She'll be on night duty, too, I expect."

***

During the drive to Mrs. Henley's, he gave vent to an occasional remark that showed he was forging the missing links in the chain.

"That theory of Ned's," he said, "the theory about the murderer being a religious monomaniac—it always struck me as a trifle far-fetched. Not only that, but it didn't seem in character for him to have invented that sort of theory on his own. He'd always struck me as a thoroughly pragmatic fellow previous to that—not at all fanciful, or given to running to alienists for their opinions."

"I wonder when he got the idea," I said. "Did he have it from the beginning, do you think? Or did it occur to him only after he committed the first few murders?"

I glanced at the Inspector and then wished I hadn't. His expression was painful to behold. "After, I'd guess," he said, after a pause. "I expect it was just coincidence that the first two or three murders were committed near places with religious names or associations. That was what I argued all along. But once the idea occurred to him, then he could make sure subsequent ones fit the same criteria. What was more, he could get credit for predicting where they might take place. That fifth murder—Matilda Bird's—he said beforehand he thought the St. Saviour's area was a likely spot. And once he had convinced the Chief of it, it gave him an excuse actually to be in the area! My God, I don't know what the Chief will say when he hears of this."

"Do you think he will believe it?" I asked. "P.C. Cobden doesn't strike me as a very convincing witness."

Inspector Harper's gaze was distant now as he contemplated this new difficulty. "I think it might be done," he said. "It will help if we can get supporting testimony from Mrs. Henley tonight. But now I think on it, there's a lot of things that would support such a theory. That night he came to the Temple of Spiritualism, for instance—the night you were attacked. He'd been patrolling on a cold, wet night, and yet he wasn't wearing an ulster or cape or any kind of overcoat. Even at the time, I remember noticing it and thinking it odd."

"You think that's significant?"

"It might be. For if he'd just killed Lizzie Gowd and gotten blood on his coat—a thing quite likely to happen, in the course of cutting a throat—he might have had to discard it or leave it somewhere to collect later. That might explain why her corpse was concealed, unlike the other victims'. He couldn't risk her being found while his coat was still nearby."

"P.C. Cobden might remember that much," I said. "Whether Inspector Freemantle was wearing an overcoat earlier and not later."

"Yes," he said, and made a note in his notebook. "I'll be sure to ask him."

"And remember how unwilling Inspector Freemantle was to believe that I was a victim of the New Moon Murderer," I said. "Nobody knew better than he that I wasn't. And," I went on, with gathering wrath, "he was actually in my bedroom! He, the New Moon murderer! *And* Miss Toth, who was a murderer, too, at least in intent."

The Inspector smiled a little at my indignation. "It's too bad, Seraphina," he said. "Two murderers in one night." His smile faded as he contemplated the idea. "And one of them a Scotland Yard detective—and he far and away the worst of the two. I don't wonder you're disgusted."

"As to that," I said, "there were two detectives there that night, too, Tom—not just two murderers. And one was flying under false colours, but the other—the other is the truest man I know. And a man whom I hold in the very highest esteem."

"Do you?" For a moment, he looked as though he would have liked to pursue this alternate subject, Dear Reader, but in the end, he contented himself with taking my hand in his own and holding it very tightly as he continued his musings on his murderous colleague.

"Toward the end, he must have seen it was getting too risky to continue. Even if he stopped, the investigation would be bound to go on. So when Toth's name came up in connection with Matilda Bird's murder, it must have seemed a God-given opportunity for him to pin his crimes on someone else. I'd take my oath that the whole business of his shadowing Toth was for no other reason than to tie the next murder to him—making it take place somewhere he'd been known to be. And bringing poor Cobden along to serve as a blind."

"But it didn't work," I said. "Absalom Toth ended up having an alibi for that night."

"But it was only for *that* night. Ned might reasonably suppose there'd be an hour or two sometime when he couldn't prove his whereabouts. That could have been another reason the body was concealed—to give him some leeway as to time."

"And that would explain why he was willing to be flexible about that murder taking place a day or two previous to the dark of the moon, when he wasn't before."

The Inspector nodded somberly. "Toth might have found it hard to prove his innocence. I hate to think of it. That a member of the force could be so corrupt—not only to murder, but to frame an innocent man for murders he himself had committed!

And I—I stood by and let it happen. That makes me complicit in the business."

I told him sternly that he was taking altogether too much credit to himself. "If you were blind to Inspector Freemantle's perfidy, then so was everyone else at Scotland Yard," I pointed out. "And some of them much blinder than you, by the sound of it."

He agreed, Dear Reader, but did not seem much comforted by the idea. "Even so, it took me a long time to get my eyes open. 'The eyes of the mind,'" he quoted, with a painful smile. "Just like in your opera."

"A case of life imitating art," I agreed. "Or vice versa. Except that here there aren't any goblins."

He shook his head. "I'm beginning to think there are goblins everywhere," he said, and lapsed into silence for the remainder of the drive.

Chapter 20

Mrs. Henley did not recognize us, which was hardly surprising. We had been dressed rather differently on our previous visit.

Appraising our gala attire with a greedy eye, she began extolling the amenities of her establishment. "The first floor front's my best—eleven shillings the night. Or if you was only wanting to stay an hour or two—"

The Inspector cut her short in his most summary manner. "I am here on police business," he said, producing his warrant once again. "We have received new information bearing on the murder of Matilda Bird."

She took a step backward, rage and disappointment written large on her face. "Not that business again!" she exclaimed. With a hint of suspicion, she added, "I never saw a policeman dressed up like a West-End swell. And who's *she*?" She turned a suspicious glare on me. "Don't say *she's* police?"

The Inspector, with admirable presence of mind, said that he was in plain-clothes, while I was a stenographer come to take down her statement. "Statement of what?" demanded Mrs. Henley. She still sounded belligerent, Dear Reader, but I thought there was apprehension in her voice, too.

The Inspector told her that he would ask the questions, thank you very much. "Is there somewhere we can speak in privacy?" he said. "I am assuming you would rather not have the whole house privy to your business."

This was clearly a home thrust. Without a word, Mrs. Henley led us into the red-plush parlour, shutting the door behind us. At first she seemed minded to let us stand, but then it apparently occurred to her that conciliation might be a better policy, for she plumped herself down in a chair and indicated that we should sit down likewise. "I'm sure I'm very happy to help the police," she said, with patent insincerity.

"Thank you," said the Inspector. "That will make my task much easier." Glancing toward me, he gave a slight nod. I opened his notebook, held the pencil at the ready, and tried to look as much like a shorthand stenographer as I could. In fact I do not know shorthand, Dear Reader, though I am accustomed to making transcripts of conversations. I hoped Mrs. Henley would not talk so fast that I could not get it all down in writing.

The Inspector's first question cut right to the heart of the matter. "Please tell me what you saw on the night of Matilda Bird's murder, when you were looking through the spyhole into her room."

"I never knew nothing about that spyhole," said Mrs. Henley promptly, "*as* I told you before. Never knew it was there at all."

"I have information that indicates otherwise," said the Inspector. "Blackmail is a serious business." He paused to let these words sink in. "We know that you use that spyhole regularly, and others like it. We have a good idea of what information you gain by doing so, and the way in which you profit by that information."

"It's a lie," said Mrs. Henley. "A dirty lie. This is a respectable house. I'd never condone such goings-on."

The Inspector held up a warning hand. "Please think before you speak, Mrs. Henley. Anything you say will be written down and may be used against you."

She threw a hunted look at me as my pencil scratched over the page. "I'm not under arrest, am I?"

"No," said the Inspector. "Of course there are multiple charges on which we *might* arrest you. But in fact we are here in your interests as much as our own. We believe you have information that might identify the murderer of Miss Bird."

"Last I heard he'd *been* identified," she shot back. "That American fellow who was arrested last week."

The Inspector looked at her sternly. "You must know very well it was not he who murdered Matilda Bird. In fact, by my calculations, you are the only person who can say with certainty who did murder her. And as long as you keep that information to yourself, your life is in danger."

As he spoke, a variety of expressions flitted over Mrs. Henley's face. Indecision was succeeded by calculation, and then resolution. "Very well," she said, rising abruptly to her feet. "I'll tell you, but I must speak to my girl first. I'll need her to keep an eye on the door while I'm in here talking to you."

After she had departed, the Inspector and I looked at each other. "Do you think—?" I began.

He gave a meaning glance at the walls and shook his head. I saw at once what he meant; likely there was a spyhole in here, too. "This is very satisfactory, Inspector," I said in a brisk, official tone. "It is gratifying to see citizens fulfilling their public duty."

He smiled, but his expression soon settled into grim lines of apprehension. I could understand why he was looking so grim. If we were right in our suppositions, he was about to hear testimony that would convict his own colleague of murder.

Mrs. Henley was gone a considerable time. We both grew uneasy, looking at each other but afraid to voice our fears. Finally, the Inspector addressed me in a whisper. "I hope she hasn't done a bunk," he said. "It didn't occur to me to keep her under guard, since we only wanted her as a witness. But perhaps it would have been better to take her in charge directly and let her make a statement down at the Yard. Only that would have been very awkward, with Ned still assigned to the case. I was hoping to get more evidence before I acted against him."

I nodded in reply, but did not dare say more. Fortunately, before many more minutes went by, Mrs. Henley returned.

She came into the room, closing the door behind her, then sat down in her chair. She took her time adjusting her skirts around her, then folded her hands in her lap and addressed us directly.

"So you think my life's in danger?" she said. "I'm sure I'm very worried to hear it—very worried indeed."

She did not sound worried, Dear Reader. I would have said rather that she sounded expectant. Again the Inspector and I exchanged glances. "Yes," he said, "if you're prepared to make a statement, ma'am, I must caution you again that your words will be written down and may be used against you."

"But not if I help arrest a murderer," she said quickly. "Isn't that right? It's not me you're wanting, it's the fellow who killed Mattie Bird?"

"That is correct," agreed the Inspector. "But I still must caution you, in duty bound."

"Ah, but we're among friends here," said a voice behind us. Turning my head, I saw Inspector Freemantle standing in the doorway to the adjoining room.

Both Inspector Harper and I were on our feet in an instant. He moved quickly to put himself between me and his colleague, and I moved quickly, too, pulling my revolver from its hidden holster, cocking it, and taking deliberate aim over his shoulder.

Inspector Freemantle was smiling, but the smile froze when he saw the revolver. "Oh," he said, rather blankly. "Not so friendly after all."

I could see calculation in his eyes as he looked from me to Inspector Harper to Mrs. Henley. "What's the meaning of this, Tom?" he said after a moment. "There seems to have been a misunderstanding." As he spoke, his right hand was moving very slowly toward his coat pocket.

"Don't move," I told him. "Stay perfectly still and keep your hands out of your pockets. I'll shoot you if you don't."

At these words, Inspector Harper threw a startled look over his shoulder and perceived the gun for the first time. His lips parted in surprise, then curved upward in a smile. "Better do what she says, Ned," he advised. Patting the pockets of his own coat, he added, "I think I've some handcuffs here somewhere."

"You shouldn't carry such vulgar things," said Inspector Fremantle reprovingly. "Not in a natty coat like that, Tom. It'll spoil the hang of it, and the set of the shoulders."

He sounded quite friendly and relaxed, Dear Reader: not worried at all. The circumstance filled me with a vague alarm. I tightened my grip on the gun, lining up the sights as carefully as I could. Even holding it in both hands, it had a tendency to sway a bit, but I thought I could hardly fail to hit him at this range.

That was where I miscalculated, Dear Reader. I had been supposing that Mrs. Henley was on *our* side, or at least grateful for our protection. But would you believe it? —while my attention was focused on Inspector Freemantle, the *maledetta bastarda* crept up beside me and suddenly wrenched the gun from my hand.

"I've got it," she announced in a jubilant voice.

"Well done," he said. "Bring it here."

I summoned up my best silly laugh. "It's not loaded," I told them both. "I'm just terribly *afraid* of guns. I know it's foolish, but I'm frightened to death just to *touch* them. I couldn't bear to put *cartridges* in one. Try it and see," I told Mrs. Henley with great earnestness. "Just point it at the floor and pull the trigger."

Instead of doing that, Dear Reader, she pointed it at me. *And* pulled the trigger.

There was a loud click and that was all.

Inspector Fremantle laughed contemptuously. "Never mind the gun," he said, "I've got a better weapon than that."

He reached again for his pocket, and after that several things happened very quickly. Inspector Harper rushed forward to seize the hand that was now holding a knife. Both men grappled for it and went down, rolling over and over as they fought for control.

Mrs. Henley, meanwhile, stood watching their struggle with avid eyes. She was still holding my gun loosely in her hand. I flung myself upon her and wrenched it away from her, then turned it butt upward and smacked her hard between the eyes. She went down with a look of astonishment and lay motionless.

Judging that she was harmless for the moment, I turned to aid Inspector Harper and was horrified to see blood staining his shirt-front. He and Inspector Freemantle were still grappling for the knife, their faces distorted and their breath coming fast. I was desperate to help, but they were struggling so closely that I was afraid of harming the wrong man.

At last there came a moment when Inspector Freemantle was uppermost. I leveled the gun at him and spoke loudly: "Stop struggling this minute, or I'll shoot you."

He did not even bother to look at me. "We already know the gun's not loaded," he said. "I'll deal with *you* in a minute."

"I think not," I said, and pulled the trigger.

The report in the closed room was deafening, Dear Reader. Inspector Freemantle rolled onto his back with a stunned look. The knife dropped from his hand, and I scooped it up, retreating a few steps. A red stain was spreading rapidly across his right shoulder. "You said it wasn't loaded!" he said.

"Silly me," I said. "I must have put cartridges in it after all." To Inspector Harper I spoke more urgently: "Tom, are you badly hurt?" I went down on my knees beside him where he lay on the floor. "O Tom, if that creature has killed you, I shall cut him into pieces with his own knife!"

It was a comfort to see a smile appear on his face. "I don't think that will be necessary, Seraphina," he said. "I'm not much injured." With an effort he sat up and pulled off his coat, grimacing as he did so.

I told him he ought to lie still until I could fetch a doctor. But he said he thought the wound was a slight one, and so it proved to be.

"*I* need a doctor," said Inspector Freemantle in an aggrieved voice. "My shoulder's bleeding like anything. I'm like to die the way it's bleeding."

I have my share of womanly sympathies, Dear Reader, but they were not excited by his words. To hear that monster whining about a bullet wound in the shoulder when he had slaughtered half a dozen women made me almost angry enough to shoot him again. It was rather Inspector Harper who told him that he would send for a doctor and who advised him kindly to lie still and not talk.

His kindness was wasted on his colleague, however. "Such nobility," sneered Inspector Freemantle. "Fair play even for the fallen enemy. I suppose you learned that at Eton and Oxford?"

Inspector Harper looked at him with pity. "The lowest constable on the beat knows that, Ned," he said, "with or without Eton and Oxford. And if police work had really been your calling, you'd know it, too."

Inspector Freemantle told him to skip the sermon. "Just fetch me a doctor," he said, "and be quick about it."

I was strongly of the opinion that, wound or no wound, he ought to be put under restraint before anything else was done. "And it wouldn't hurt to search him, either, Tom," I urged. "After all, he might have more than one weapon. If he tries to hurt you while you're doing it," I added, in a voice loud enough to reach his ears, "I shall shoot him again."

"Ah, so you have *more* cartridges in that unloaded gun," said Inspector Harper with detached interest. "Very well, then. Just don't use them unless you need to."

I didn't need to, Dear Reader. Inspector Freemantle submitted sullenly to being searched and then restrained. He proved to be carrying a pair of handcuffs of his own, which was convenient. Because of his shoulder wound, Inspector Harper did not like to handcuff his wrists together, so he secured one wrist to the leg of Mrs. Henley's imitation mahogany breakfront and the other to a heavy chair. His ankles he tied together using his own white neckcloth. I was sorry to see it put to such a base use.

At this point Mrs. Henley was showing signs of reviving, so I suggested she ought to be restrained, too. Initially I thought I would have to sacrifice my stockings (silk, brand new, and ten shillings the pair) for the purpose, but luckily I recollected that she was wearing stockings, too. Inspector Harper averted his eyes modestly as I removed her shoes and stripped the stockings from her legs. I felt I had never loved him more than at that moment.

We had another short conference regarding who should go fetch a doctor and constable. He suggested I should do it, first loaning him my gun so he might stand guard over the prisoners. But I explained that a woman liked to keep her staff of power in her own hands. "Besides, Tom, he thinks *you* wouldn't shoot him if it was you standing guard. He knows *I* would. You go."

***

After he had left, there was silence in the room. Mrs. Henley still appeared to be unconscious, but I sat down on a chair where I could keep an eye on her as well as Inspector Freemantle and held my revolver at the ready.

Inspector Freemantle lay still, his eyes fixed on me, breathing with an effort. "I can't believe you shot me," he said presently. "You, a woman!"

"I'm sure that seems very ironic," I agreed.

"And a whore!"

"No, you're wrong there," I said. "Although I admit it would be a beautiful piece of poetic justice."

Inspector Freemantle moved restlessly and did not immediately answer. "I didn't intend for you to come into it," he said after a bit. "That wasn't any of my doing. Him, though—I was afraid all along he suspected me."

"Inspector Harper?" I asked.

He nodded. "I was afraid he suspected me," he repeated. "After that business last month, I could see the way he looked at me. I had to do something to throw him off the track."

I was fascinated by this glimpse into his thought processes, Dear Reader. I knew very well that Inspector Harper had never suspected him at all—not until this evening, at any rate. It was his own guilt that had made him fear he was on the verge of being discovered. "I suppose framing poor Absalom Toth was your way of throwing him off track?" I asked.

A faint smile appeared on his face. "Yes. Came pretty close to doing it, too."

"You were the one who tipped off the *Banner*, of course?"

His smile was answer enough, Dear Reader. Gradually, however, it gave way to a look of bitterness. "It didn't answer, though. Here I am, likely to hang if I don't bleed to death first. And all for killing a lot of whores." He looked at me aggressively. "I shouldn't be punished for killing whores. I ought to get a medal, by jingo. Better if the whole lot of them were dead, damnable pox-ridden vermin that they are."

Enlightenment dawned on me. "I suppose one of them gave you a venereal disease," I said. "Good God, is that what this is all about? It hardly seems a sufficient reason to kill the poor things. You might have contented yourself with retaliating in kind and simply passing the infection along."

As I spoke, his face was distorted by a spasm of rage and pain. "Oh, I *see*," I said. "Not *able* to pass it on. Permanently incapacitated, I suppose? That would explain why there wasn't any sexual connection with the victims."

His answer was a string of abuse, Dear Reader. I used it as an opportunity to practice my Italian vocabulary. Together we made a sort of duet, or perhaps recitative would be the proper term.

By now Mrs. Henley was starting to stir. She began complaining as soon as she opened her eyes: "What am *I* tied up for? *I'm* not a criminal! I'm a respectable businesswoman, I am."

"Who's been conspiring with a murderer," I said. "Would you mind telling me, ma'am, as a matter of curiosity, why you would league yourself with such a man? It seems a dangerous thing to do, on the face of it. Even if you had evidence that would convict him of murder, you couldn't be sure he wouldn't murder you, too."

"Ah, Peg and I understand each other," said Inspector Freemantle, with a ghastly semblance of his old jaunty manner.

"I don't care about nothing but my business," said Mrs. Henley sullenly. "Whatever he's done, it's nothing to do with me."

"I think I understand," I said. "I remember now that it was *you—*" I looked at Inspector Freemantle, "—who spoke against arresting her, or closing down her house. Ostensibly to give her enough rope to hang herself, but really as a reward for keeping quiet about your murdering Miss Bird."

"I don't care about nothing but my business," affirmed Mrs. Henley.

"I can see that," I said. "But I still think you were taking a risk, ma'am. Even if you'd kept your side of the bargain, I suspect you might have been found dead with your throat cut, too, one of these days."

Inspector Freemantle winked at me.

Mrs. Henley merely repeated that she didn't care about anything but her business. I was relieved when I heard heavy steps in the hall, heralding the arrival of the police.

Chapter 21

What struck me most about Inspector Freemantle's arrest was its solemnity, Dear Reader. It might have been rather a funeral service. From the pair of young constables in their helmets and tunics, to the elderly superintendent hurried out of bed and into his clothes to preside over the business, to my own particular detective inspector, every man of them wore a stricken look, as he might have done if his colleague had died in service rather than being hauled off in disgrace.

"This is a bad business," the superintendent kept saying, "a very bad business." He repeated himself quite as much as Mrs. Henley, Dear Reader. In particular he questioned and cross-questioned Inspector Harper as to the exact circumstances that had led him to suspect his colleague of being the New Moon Murderer. "What the newspapers will say, I don't know," he said, shaking his head. "I doubt we can hush it up. At the very least, the Home Secretary will have to know. This is a bad business."

About the time he remarked that Inspector Harper would have to go down to the Yard and make a full reporting to the Chief Commissioner, I felt obliged to step in.

"He is *wounded*," I said fiercely. "He had to defend his life against that monster. And in the process he was *stabbed*. And he has had no chance for a doctor to even *look* at his wound. And you've already taken down everything he has to say, two or three times over. If you don't let him go right now to rest and recover, I shall write to the newspapers *myself*."

"God bless my soul," exclaimed the superintendent, looking taken aback by this address. He appeared to be a kind man at heart, however, for he told the Inspector that he certainly ought to see to his wound right away and then get some rest. "You've done well, Mr. Harper," he said. "We appreciate your efforts in bringing this business to a close. God knows I could wish it had had a different close, but there's no help for that. You needn't come in before afternoon. We'll be a long time sifting through this business, and I daresay we can manage without you for that long."

I carried the Inspector triumphantly off in a cab. "A ministering angel thou," he quoted with a faint smile.[16] "You know it's only a scratch, Seraphina."

"I daresay," I said, "but you'd better see to it all the same."

"It'll be well enough if I just rest it on the way," he said.

By "rest it," he apparently meant putting his arm around me and leaning his head against mine. It seemed an eminently sensible precaution.

When we reached the Temple, I used my latch key to let us in. There was only a single lamp burning in the front window. The

---

[16]"Oh, Woman, in our hour of ease/Uncertain, coy, and hard to please/And variable as the shade/As the light quivering aspen made/When pain and sorrow crease our brow/A ministering angel thou!" Sir Walter Scott's verse is traditionally quoted at women in these sort of situations, *ad nauseum—Ed.*

place was deserted, and after a moment I recalled that Susan was gone on her mysterious business. I lit a few more lamps, took the Inspector into the Sitting Room, put him on the sofa, and fetched him a brandy-and-soda. I had one, too, feeling I deserved it at that point.

He accepted the glass, but did not drink immediately. Instead, he sat holding it in his hands and looking down at it as though he did not know what to do with it. "You look tired to death, Tom," I said. "And no wonder. If you would like to lie down, I will fetch a pillow and eiderdown to make you more comfortable."

He thanked me, but said it wasn't that kind of tiredness. "In fact, I don't know that I'm tired at all."

"Distressed," I suggested. "Distraught. And no wonder. It's a terrible thing to have one's trust betrayed in that way, by one's own colleague."

"Yes," he agreed. "Not unprecedented, however. To use a little of that university education Ned objected to, '*Quis custodiet ipsos custodes?*' With rather a bitter smile, he translated: "Who will watch the watchman?"

I pointed out that Inspector Freemantle was a glaring exception to the general rule of policemen. He received my words with an impatient shake of his head. "I should have known," he said. "Known it much sooner, at any rate. Known it without having it thrust under my nose."

"He thought you did know it," I said. "Don't you see, Tom? He thought you knew because he judged you by his own standard. And you never supposed he was guilty because you were judging him by *yours*."

"Is that supposed to be a comfort?" he asked. I was relieved to see that his expression was now one of wry amusement.

"It ought to be," I said firmly.

"Well, perhaps it will be, in time." He took a drink from his glass and sat musing a while longer. "It's curious. I don't seem to feel it—at least, not yet. The whole business seems unreal. Like something on a stage." He flashed me a quick smile. "Like your opera this evening. Was that only this evening? It seems a hundred years ago."

I said it seemed that way to me, too.

"None of it seemed real," he went on, "except, perhaps, for the moment when that woman pointed the gun at you and pulled the trigger. *That* seemed real enough." He drew a deep breath. "I can still feel it this minute when I remember it—thinking you were going to die."

With feeling, I said that that moment still seemed pretty fresh in my mind, too. He turned a searching gaze upon me.

"How could you know?" he asked. "I saw the gun—handled it myself while you were busy tying her up. It's a six-chamber revolver. But you only had five cartridges in it. How could you know to leave the one chamber empty?" With an attempt at levity, he added, "If the Spirits told you to arrange it that way beforehand, I take off my hat to them."

I was a little shaken to realize this was almost the literal truth, Dear Reader. I had acquired the revolver years ago, while touring the American West. My tutor in its use had been a gentleman who had achieved fame as a gun-fighter in those turbulent times. The measure of leaving an empty chamber under the hammer had been one he recommended, for if the revolver were accidentally dropped, or the trigger squeezed before it was clear of the holster, no harm would be done. It was only necessary to squeeze it twice instead of once to move past the vacant chamber.

Following some events which are no concern of this narrative, I had parted ways with this gentleman and soon after had heard that he had passed into the Summerland. It had been a shock but not a surprise, Dear Reader. Men of his profession are not typically long-lived.

I told the Inspector an expurgated version of this story, but as usual, he seemed to see a little more than I had told him. "Was this when you were in San Francisco?" he inquired.

"Who told you I was ever in San Francisco?" I demanded.

He merely shook his head.

I thought it as well to change the subject. "Well," I said, "if we are to talk of moments that curdle the blood, I will say that when I saw you struggling with him on the floor, and then saw you were bleeding . . . I thought he had killed you."

For the life of me, I could not keep the tears from my eyes. This circumstance seemed to afford the Inspector satisfaction. He put an arm around me again and drew me close to him.

"It beat anything I ever saw on a stage," he said. "You were very bloodthirsty in my defence. Would you really have cut him to pieces with his own knife?"

"I might have," I said. "If he had killed you, I might have done anything."

"Well," he said, "I'm glad it didn't work out that way." He put the other arm around me, too, and drew me closer. After a moment, with a seriousness that belied his words, he said, "I'd much rather be with you here and now, not frolicking in the Summerland."

I made a noise of assent.

He touched my tiara (which I was still wearing), stroked the fabric of my dress, and smiled. "I shall never forget it," he went on. "Seeing you in that preposterous dress . . . sweeping down on him like an avenging angel."

Rather incoherently, I gave him to understand that I wasn't any kind of an angel. "Nonsense," he said. "You must let me be the judge of that." And then he kissed me.

I don't know whether it was the dress, or the opera, or the near escape from death, or all of them put together, but events unfolded rather quickly after that, Dear Reader. I kept thinking that he would draw back, but he didn't. And then, finally, it was too late to draw back, and after that I had something else to think about.

***

There is something to be said for age and experience. Young couples who imagine they hold a monopoly on the pleasures of love are much mistaken.

I was able to confirm that the Inspector's former reticence had nothing to do with incapacity.

I was also forced to recant my statement that the English are cold.

And finally, I was able to note that, while there are plenty of experiences in life that fail to live up to one's expectations, now and again there is one that is truly transcendental.

I shall never look at the Sitting Room sofa in the same way again.

***

Eventually we reached a point where I was able to articulate all these things, in the expansive way one does at such moments. Raising himself on his elbows, he studied me carefully—and rather questioningly, I thought.

"What wilt thou, love?" I inquired, and went on to add in a reckless manner that he might make any request, even unto half of the kingdom.

He smiled. "May I? Well, then—I was wondering if you might like to marry me."

He certainly knew to strike while the iron was hot. "Oh," I said weakly. "Marry you."

It didn't actually sound distasteful at that moment, Dear Reader. Few things would have, to be sure. "Do you feel it's *necessary*?" I asked—not in any complaining spirit, but rather out of curiosity. "I can see it must mean a great deal to you, Tom, but I'm not sure I understand why."

"It does mean a great deal to me. It means *everything* to me. And I think," he said, looking into my eyes, "it must mean something to you, too. Or you wouldn't be so opposed to it."

"Yes," I said, after a moment. "It frightens me—the irrevocability of it. One can't know beforehand if one is making a mistake."

"That must be the only thing that ever did frighten you," he said, smiling but looking a little sad, too. "You already know I don't want your money or property, Seraphina. You needn't take my name, and you needn't promise to obey me. We both know that's not on the cards, and I wouldn't want you to perjure yourself. We needn't even live together. I can stay on with Mrs. MacIntyre—"

"That woman," I said with loathing.

He went on, disregarding the interruption. "I can stay on with Mrs. MacIntyre. We can see each other when it's convenient for us both, just as we do now. I wouldn't be able to make many demands on you in any case, given the nature of my job."

I took a deep breath. "But don't you think *you* might regret it?" I said. "Here you are, likely to be made Chief Inspector for the brilliant way you solved the case of the New Moon Murderer—"

"Which I could never have done without *you*," he put in swiftly.

"—and you want to saddle yourself with a wife who is—well, who at the very least isn't entirely respectable. Who is . . . perhaps . . . criminal, even," I said, determined to make a clean breast of the matter.

He said he wanted nothing more. "It's a bargain I am quite prepared to make. But—" he gestured ruefully toward our entangled bodies, "I'm afraid I haven't anything left to bargain with."

I intimated he had plenty to bargain with, at which he underwent a sudden change of mood. "Put on your clothes, woman," he ordered, "and come and be married. And then we'll see if I can't improve on my previous performance."

"Not possible," I told him.

"You think not?" he said, with a light of challenge in his eyes.

"Not possible to be married," I explained. "Although I tend to doubt the other, too. But married at this hour? Don't be ridiculous, Tom."

The gleam in his eye was more pronounced. "Do you care to make a wager on it?"

I felt quite assured of taking his money, Dear Reader. I put on my clothes again—they were only half off, in any case—and tidied my hair before the glass. The false hair had not come completely unmoored, I was pleased to see. He helped me with the hairpins, and the corset strings, and the buttons up the back of my dress. In return, I sponged the blood from his shirt and bandaged his knife-wound. There was a nice, intimate domesticity about it all. I found myself almost sorry we weren't going to be married. But I reckoned I was safe enough. It was ridiculous to suppose he could find a clergyman willing to perform the marriage service at this hour.

He summoned a cabman from around the corner, and we drove to a little cottage in Paddington—evidently a parsonage. A sleepy-looking maidservant appeared in answer to his knock. The Inspector gave her his card and stated, "I need the services of Dr. Ames. He will know what it is in reference to."

Presently Dr. Ames appeared, his surplice hastily donned, and his wife at his elbow. They were both elderly people, and they both wore the foolish, sentimental smiles people wear when a marriage is about to be perpetrated.

I saw I had underestimated the Inspector's resolve—or his guile. But I still reckoned I was safe. Even if the clergyman were willing to marry us here and now, it would require a special license, which could only be obtained after much expense and bother.

As I was reflecting on this point, the Inspector produced a paper from his breast pocket. Dr. Ames inspected it, then smiled benevolently at us both over his spectacles. "This appears to be quite in order," said. "Just step into the parlour, if you please."

I reckoned I was still safe, Dear Reader. For even if we went through the marriage service, *Seraphina Fox is not my real name.* I would not have to regard the marriage as legally binding unless I wanted to. I comforted myself with this reflection, right up until the moment when Dr. Ames said, "Do you, Mary Marion, take this man to be your lawful wedded husband?"

I flashed the Inspector a look of reproach. His expression was unrepentant, Dear Reader—quite jubilant, in fact. It was, as Felicity might say, a fair cop.

"Yes," I said resentfully. "Yes, I will."

Chapter 22

After the ceremony, the Ames insisted that we stay to breakfast. They were the best kind of Christians, Dear Reader: kind and generous and not at all narrow-minded. Both of them admired my dress in the most innocent way. And when I apologetically mentioned the source of its inspiration, we had a most interesting conversation about the religious customs of the ancient Canaanites.

Afterwards, the Inspector and I rode back to the Temple. The sun was just rising, casting a roseate glow over the oily waters of the Thames. It wasn't Walden Pond, perhaps, but it struck me as being very beautiful.

I took the Inspector up to my bedroom, where he set himself to winning the other part of our wager. It gave me a very favourable view of married life at the outset. I am ashamed to say I forgot all about his knife-wound, and so did he. He ended up bleeding all over my sheets. It was, in the event, quite allegorical.

As he had to go to work that afternoon, I didn't get a chance to tax him with his stratagem until evening. He was quite as unrepentant then as earlier.

"You don't think," I suggested, "that it was taking me at a disadvantage? Working on my womanly sensibilities at a time when they were already disordered and vulnerable to suggestion?"

He explained very seriously that when dealing with a character like mine, a man needed every advantage he could get.

"Providing yourself beforehand with a special license, too," I fumed. "And making arrangements with a clergyman. You must have been very sure of yourself, Tom!"

He said that he had only been hopeful. "I was counting on your being generous in victory," he explained.

"And that business of my *name*—!"

"I won't call you it in public," he assured me. "It will be our secret. *Mary*," he whispered into my ear.

It sent a little shiver down my spine. I had always thought it a dull name, Dear Reader—quite pedestrian, in fact. But it appears that this, as so much else, is a matter of context.

He then surprised me by asking if I would like to accompany him to Paris. "I've received the promotion to Chief Inspector. And it looks as though I'll be obliged to visit the Sûreté on some business next month. If you came along with me, we might stay on a week or two after the business is done and make a proper honeymoon of it."

I adore Paris, Dear Reader. The idea of visiting that city in his company left me speechless with delight. It was only for a moment, however, and then my face fell. "I'm not certain that's a good idea, Tom," I said hesitantly.

The fact is, Dear Reader, that I had passed a few years in Paris at an earlier period of my life. And I had reason to think the Sûreté might not welcome me back very hospitably—or rather, that they might be entirely *too* hospitable and perhaps even find accommodation for me, at government expense.

The Inspector regarded me with a carefully neutral expression. "If you're thinking about that business with the Lavoisier will," he said, "I've been making inquiries, and it seems the family has given up any idea of prosecuting. In any case," he went on, with a glimmer of a smile, "as my wife you would naturally be above suspicion."

Of course he was perfectly right, Dear Reader. It was, by itself, almost enough to reconcile me to the married state. As Mrs. Thomas Harper, I might pass unremarked among the hordes of English visitors to the City of Lights. I could envisage exactly the kind of matronly bonnet I would wear.

The Inspector broke in on these reflections with an apologetic cough. "But it might be as well if you didn't visit San Francisco again any time soon," he said.

It appeared he hadn't wanted to buy a pig in a poke, either, Dear Reader. I was too happy about visiting Paris again to hold it against him.

***

As for the New Moon Murderer, it remains to be seen whether the public will ever learn his true identity. At present the higher officials at Scotland Yard, together with the Home Secretary, seem inclined to hush the matter up. There can be no doubt that the idea of a policeman having committed such atrocities would rebound against the whole force. This would be true even if Inspector Freemantle succeeds in claiming insanity as a defence, as appears to be his strategy. His pet alienist has come out in favour of the theory—and in fact it seems that the venereal illness from which he suffers does often result in mental derangement.

As regards his real motive in the crimes, I was perfectly correct, Dear Reader. A disease caught from a prostitute had rendered him sexually incapable. If one wishes to be strictly accurate, however, it was the *treatment* for the disease that did the real damage. He had the misfortune to fall into the hands of a medical practitioner who was as great a butcher as he was, and this so-called doctor put him through a horrifying course of treatment that ended in amputation of the diseased member. Even I will admit that a man might bear a grudge after such an experience, though to my mind, it would have been more rational to have visited his resentment on the medical profession rather than Woman Unfortunates.

Such diseases are, it appears, astonishingly prevalent, and not only among Unfortunates. This is another idea to reconcile me to marriage and monogamy.[17] Just because I was fortunate enough in the past not to incur disease—or a suit for criminal intercourse—doesn't mean I would always be so lucky. As Susan says, the pitcher goes to the well once too often.

Speaking of Susan, Dear Reader, I continue to worry about her. She came back from her holiday looking easier in her mind, but I can tell that some disquiet remains. It looks as though I may be obliged to conduct a discreet investigation into her affairs.

There is always something to worry about in this world.

---

[17] It would appear from this statement that Madame Fox does not regard the two as necessarily synonymous.—*Ed.*

At any rate, I don't need to worry about the Toths any longer. Absalom Toth was freed with apologies immediately after the arrest of Inspector Freemantle, and Mrs. Toth responded by shaking the dust of England from her feet. She and her family are back in the States now, and I understand she has plans to start her own transcendental vegetarian commune, which will doubtless end as all such ventures do.[18] I don't miss her or her family, Dear Reader, but I do miss Henry David Thoreau. One seldom encounters so fresh and original a Spirit at the séance table.

Thankfully, my operatic venture has proved so lucrative that I do not miss the income I received from the Toths. It is true that the critical reviews for *Night and Day* have been rather mixed—the *Banner*, for one, taking exception to what it called the show's "subversive themes." But it has enjoyed a great popular success. You can hardly walk down a London street without hearing a hurdy-gurdy playing, "Do You Not Dream?"

Mr. Hinney was so pleased by the receipts that he has proposed our collaborating on another, similar venture. It appears that Bellini, Donizetti, and quite a few other famous composers left unfinished works behind, which might profitably be completed with Spiritual assistance. It is a tempting idea, Dear Reader. I told Mr. Hinney I would think about it.

In the course of our conversation, he also mentioned that he was thinking about electrifying the opera house. I was surprised when he asked my advice on the subject. It would

[18] *I.e.*, badly. Witness the Fruitlands commune of the 1840s. The debility and early death of Lizzie Alcott, the real-life counterpart of Beth in *Little Women*, was an indirect result of this venture.—*Ed.*

appear that he has guessed the secret of the Spiritograph. But I don't expect he will betray me. As fellow theatre people, we both have a stake in keeping the public ignorant and credulous.

My chief concern at present is to balance the needs of my business with those of my changed marital status. For the present, Inspector Harper remains with Mrs. MacIntyre, a solution which satisfies none of us. Yet I hesitate to openly introduce the complication of a husband into my household. Indeed, the Inspector and I have both lived independently so long that it is a question whether cohabitation might not prove as unsatisfactory as our present arrangement.

Just when I was at my wits' end to resolve the dilemma, a solution unexpectedly appeared. After long negotiation, the owner of my building has finally agreed to sell to me. This means that I will own not only the Temple of Spiritualism but the two flats and dental office which also occupy the premises.

The bedroom of one of these flats adjoins my own on the second floor. It strikes me that the same workmen who installed the door in the wainscoting of my Spirit Parlour might perfectly well do the same in the wall between the two bedrooms.

There is something delightful about the idea of one's husband visiting one in this manner. One gathers that married life is prone to pall upon long acquaintance. This kind of expedient might help keep the novelty fresh, and it would also enable me to keep a close eye on him and his affairs. There is a place in this world for idealists like him, but I strongly feel that idealism does better when it is mediated with realism, practicality, and a touch of equivocation. And mediation is my business, Dear Reader, as you know—none better.

"*Quis custodiet ipsos custodes?*" Who will watch the watchman?

I will, that's who.

The End

About the Author

Joy Reed is the author of 16 romance novels, an award-winning master's thesis, and the Seraphina Fox mystery series. Her works have been published around the world and translated into four languages. She is a voracious and indiscriminate reader, a collector of unconsidered trifles, and a historian specializing in the Bleeding Kansas era. Ms. Reed lives with her long-suffering husband and an undisclosed number of cats and tarantulas in the Greater Little Rock area.

You can read her musings about life and literature on her blog BookJoy: http://bookjoy.livejournal.com/

www.ingramcontent.com/pod-product-compliance
Lightning Source LLC
Chambersburg PA
CBHW031317170626
46807CB00002B/447

* 9 7 8 0 6 9 2 1 1 6 1 8 0 *